"Oof!" She slammed into Leo, the nose tackle on the school football team.

Whoever had been trailing her vanished, leaving just a fleeting black shadow behind a couple walking arm in arm.

"Did you see who was following me?" she asked, trying to peer around Leo.

"Yeah," Leo answered with a snort. "Me!"

"Not you," Sudi said. "Someone dressed all in black has been trying to sneak up on me all day."

Taller than anyone in the hallway, Leo easily scanned the crowd. "No one's wearing all black."

His answer sent a chill through Sudi. If the shadow wasn't another student, then maybe something more deadly was stalking her. Only a few months back, she would have laughed and figured it was all a figment of her imagination. But things had quickly changed. She now knew firsthand that dangerous supernatural forces really did exist.

Head down, she kept walking, her attention focused on her peripheral vision. When friends called her name and shouted for her to wait up, she pretended not to hear them.

She had gone only a short distance when the

CHAPTER 1

Sudi couldn't ignore the creeping sensation that someone was following her through the crowded hallways of Lincoln High School. Since earlier that day, she had been catching glimpses of a figure from out of the corner of her eye—a dark blur prowling behind the other students.

She waited patiently, determined to find out who was stalking her, and this time, when the phantom-shadow closed in, she took a deep breath and spun around, ready to give chase.

For my dear friend
Caron Lee Cohen

SISTERS
of
ISIS

4

The Haunting

LYNNE EWING

HYPERION/NEW YORK

An Imprint of Disney Book Group

Published by Hyperion Books for Children, an imprint of
Disney Book Group. No part of this book may be reproduced
or transmitted in any form or by any means, electronic or
mechanical, including photocopying, recording, or by any
information or storage retrieval system, without written
permission from the publisher. For information, please address
Hyperion Books for Children, 114 Fifth Avenue, New York,
New York 10011-5690.

Printed in the United States of America
First Edition
1 3 5 7 9 10 8 6 4 2
This book is set in 12-point Griffo Classico.
Reinforced binding
Library of Congress Cataloging-in-Publication Data on file
ISBN 978-1-4231-0842-9

www.hyperionteens.com

unsettling feeling of being watched crept over her again. She braced herself and looked around. This time, she spied Zack.

He stood near the front door, staring at her. Since she had learned his secret, he and his friends had begun harassing her; it was just one more problem in her complicated life. Sudi noticed his constant companions, Garrett and Nick, weren't with him now, so maybe they had been the ones following her. Two people trailing after her would explain how the shadowy figure had been able to disappear and then reappear so quickly in another place.

One problem solved. But she still had to deal with Zack. He wouldn't let her leave school, not without—

She silenced her thoughts and started back, retracing her steps. Students jostled her as she bumped and shoved against the flow in the overcrowded hallway.

After pausing to make sure no one was watching her, she stole into an empty classroom, walked quickly to the far side of the teacher's desk, and sat down on the floor, hidden from anyone who might peek in. If she waited long enough, perhaps Zack and his friends would think she had already left school and give up their chase.

She had thought about reporting them to the vice principal, but even if she had, would he even have believed her? She barely believed the truth herself. Anyone listening to her complaint would have thought she was lying or on something. Teachers loved Zack—he was a good student— serious, intent, and Harvard-bound. No one would have believed he was part of a group that worshipped an arcane Egyptian god.

Taking deep breaths, she tried to force herself to relax and think about something else. Zack and his friends weren't her only problem. Scott had stopped returning her calls. She couldn't imagine what she had done to upset him that much. But maybe the way he had been ignoring her explained her sudden attraction to Raul, the new guy at school. His father was with Argentina's diplomatic corps. Sudi wondered if Raul knew how to tango. Then, imagining her body tight against his, she beat out the duple rhythm of the dance with her fingers on the dusty floor.

When the noise in the hallway finally subsided,

she left her hiding place and opened the door a crack, anxious to find Sara. They had a *sumi-e* art class that evening.

With slow, furtive steps, she joined the other stragglers.

Immediately, Garrett and Nick rounded the corner, smiling slyly.

"Hey, Sudi," Garrett said as his feet struck the floor with light, quick steps. He'd won the last Dance Dance Revolution tournament, and now Sudi and her friends laughed at the way he walked everywhere by moving his feet in an intricate pattern, as if an invisible pad with four arrows pointing up, down, left, and right lay under his feet.

Falling in step beside her, Nick chuckled, "You were in that classroom for a really long time. What were you doing?"

"Homework," she shot back, hating the fact that the entire time that she had thought she was safely hidden, they had been waiting for her.

Striding quickly, she tried to outpace them. When that didn't work, she turned abruptly and ran right into Zack.

She tried to move around him, but he continued to block her way. "Why'd you run away from me, Sudi?" Zack smirked. "Didn't you see me waiting for you at the front door?"

His intense look held too much promise of something bad. She tried to edge away from him, but when she did, Nick and Garrett pressed against her, hemming her in.

"I thought you and I were friends," Zack continued.

"We were once," she admitted, "but I hate what you've become."

She tried to pinpoint when the change had taken place. She should have noticed—there must have been some clue—but she couldn't do anything about it now.

"Feeling guilty?" he whispered, seeming to read her mind. "I know a way you can make it up to me."

When he tried to touch her hair, she slapped his hand away. Her earring caught in his fingers and fell to the floor. He looked down at the scattered beads, and then his eyes returned to hers, his expression cold and unreadable.

After a long pause, he said, "Three against one, Sudi. Do you really think you can win?"

Garrett laughed.

This time, when Zack reached up to touch her, Sudi cringed but didn't fight him.

Then, gently, seductively, he brushed back her hair and traced the birthmark hidden on her scalp.

"Descendant," he whispered, awestruck, his breath sweet and warm against her face.

Nick and Garrett leaned over her, straining to see the mark.

"Royal blood," Nick said, but there was no mocking in his tone this time.

Sudi had always thought the birthmark was just an oddly shaped mole. Now, she knew it was the sacred eye of Horus, which identified her as a Descendant.

"Why don't you show us your magic?" Zack asked as his fingers slid down her cheek. He cupped the side of her face before his hand continued down and rested around her neck. His fingers and thumb closed tightly.

Garrett and Nick watched, eager to see what Sudi would do.

"Use your power," Zack urged.

Instead, Sudi glared up at him, refusing to cough or gag. Blood swelled uncomfortably in her veins.

"I can feel your heart beating," Zack said softly, challenging her outward show of bravery. "It's racing with fear. Are you afraid of what I've become?"

"You know she is," Garrett snickered. His toe tapped noisily, revealing his excitement.

Sudi clutched her purse strap so hard her fingers ached. "My heart beats fast when I look at spiders, too."

Leaning down, close to her face, Zack whispered into her ear, "You hate bugs. I remember. I used to chase you around the playground, scaring you with the beetles and crickets I caught."

Footsteps echoed down the hallway, and Zack snapped to attention.

"Sudi!" a familiar voice called.

Taking a step back, Zack smiled. "Sooner or later, we'll finish our talk." The tone, more than the words, conveyed a warning.

Rubbing her neck, Sudi turned.

Sara ran toward her, a Coke in one hand and a

tablet of *gasenshi* rice paper in the other. "We have art class tonight, did you forget?"

"No, I just got . . ."—Sudi searched for a word—"detained."

"You're trembling." Sara handed Sudi her Coke. "I hope you didn't go all day without eating again. You have to be more careful. Last week you almost passed out in science lab." Then a curious expression crossed her face and she looked around, seeming to sense something like a residue of bad emotion left over from the confrontation. "What happened?"

Sudi glanced around. Zack had disappeared; Nick stood in front of an open locker, pulling out books; and Garrett was spinning on his heels. "Nothing." She took the soft drink and swallowed, surprised that her mouth and throat had become so dry.

"Come on," Sara said, still looking unsettled. "We've been waiting for you."

"We?" Sudi asked.

"Sorry." Sara shrugged and started walking. "Michelle enrolled online. She's going to the class with us."

Sudi felt her shoulders slump. After Sara's

Sweet Sixteen had been such a huge success, Michelle had decided that Sara was *her* best friend.

"I can't focus with Michelle around," Sudi complained. She wanted to concentrate on her painting, not listen to Michelle's gossip. "That was one of the reasons I signed up for the class in the first place," she explained, "because *sumi-e* is also a form of meditation."

"I know," Sara sighed. "Me and my big mouth. I should never have told Michelle about the class. She copies everything we do." Then, abruptly changing the subject, she added, "Zack is so cute."

Sudi followed Sara's love-struck gaze. Zack stood at the front entrance, leaning against the wall. How did he get there so quickly? Without passing Sudi and Sara in the hallway?

"Impossible," Sudi breathed.

"I know," Sara said. "He's impossibly good-looking, isn't he?"

"Jeez, not you, too," Sudi said.

"I know, everyone's crushing on him." Sara stood up a little straighter. "He's turned from an ugly duckling into this incredible hottie. What did he do?"

"You don't want to know," Sudi replied bitterly. Then, she stopped Sara and stepped in front of her. When they were face to face, Sudi said, "We've been best friends forever, so if I tell you to do something, can you just trust me and do what I say without asking a bunch of questions?"

Sara smiled excitedly. "Of course. What do you want me to do?"

"Stay away from Zack," Sudi said.

Frowning, Sara said, "You're joking."

Sudi shook her head. "Not."

Walking together again at a slower pace, they both stared at Zack.

"I've got to ask," Sara said, still looking straight ahead. "I've never heard anyone say anything bad about him. So why should I stay away from him? What do you know?"

"I can't tell you," Sudi replied. Her throat tightened, and the unpleasant heaviness returned to her chest.

Zack was now walking toward them with slow, lazy steps.

"Hey!" He put on his friendliest smile for Sara. "I've been looking for you."

"You have?" Sara stared up at him and cocked her head in a flirty way. Her long black hair spilled over her shoulder.

"We have to hurry," Sudi reminded her. "You said Michelle was waiting for us."

"Go on," Sara said to Sudi, but her eyes never left Zack. "I'll catch up with you guys."

Sudi gave Sara a pleading look, which Sara promptly ignored.

Reluctantly, Sudi walked on ahead and waited down the hall for her friend. She leaned back against the wall and closed her eyes, longing for her old life, and remembering the night Abdel had summoned her. It wasn't a happy memory.

Abdel belonged to a secret society called the Hour priests. Back in ancient times, the goddess Isis had given the priests the Book of Thoth and told them to watch the night skies. When the stars warned of danger, the priests were supposed to find the next Descendants and give them the book, because only the divine heirs to the throne of Egypt, those marked with the sacred eye of Horus, had the power to use the magic.

Sudi hadn't believed Abdel; neither had Dalila

nor Meri, the girls who had been summoned with Sudi. But too much had happened for her to deny the truth now. She was a Descendant, destined to stand against evil and defend the world.

And, unfortunately, that meant fighting the Cult of Anubis. The cult ran a popular spa in Washington, D.C., and had recently opened a teen club called The Jackal. Most residents dismissed the cult as some kind of new-age group, but Sudi knew its true history.

In ancient Egypt, Anubis had been the most important funerary god until the god's cult had been taken over by priests devoted to Osiris. Instead of surrendering their power, a few of the priests who had served Anubis turned to the evil god Seth. Determined to destroy the bloodline of Horus and return the universe to the chaos from which it came, they used Anubis and the Book of Gates in unholy ways.

Zack had joined the cult, knowing what it was. Sudi's onetime friend was her enemy now.

Someone nudged Sudi. She gasped and opened her eyes, jolted from her thoughts.

"I didn't mean to scare you." Sara stood in

front of her. "What were you daydreaming about?"

"Just stuff," Sudi answered.

"Stuff, huh?" Sara started toward the exit. "I bet you were thinking about Scott."

"Yeah," Sudi mumbled, wishing she could tell Sara the truth, wishing she could tell her everything about Zack—then maybe she'd take her advice.

Together, the girls pushed through the front door. A blast of wind hit them as they stepped outside.

Michelle waved and walked over to them, her hair perfect and lips glossy. She wore mammoth sunglasses, even though the sun had slid behind a mass of gray clouds.

"What took you so long?" she asked, hooking arms with Sudi and Sara and guiding them toward her town car.

The driver opened the back door.

"I can't go," Sudi whispered, loosening Michelle's grip on her arm. She didn't want to spend more time competing with Michelle for Sara's friendship. "I just remembered that I have—"

"Don't tell me you have to go over to Abdel's again," Sara groaned. "You're always visiting him.

What's so important that you have to miss class?"

"It's not that," Sudi stammered, trying to find an excuse that wouldn't hurt Sara's feelings. "I have too much homework."

"You're not fooling me," Michelle said.

"I'm not?" Sudi looked at Michelle, but when she did, her own reflection stared back at her from the black lenses of Michelle's sunglasses.

"I hate girls who hurry home and sit by the phone, waiting for their boyfriends to call," Michelle said.

"I'm not going home to wait for a call," Sudi argued.

"Please," Michelle huffed. "I've played that waiting game. It's a waste of time. Scott's never going to return your calls."

Sudi shot Sara a look.

"I didn't say anything," Sara squealed.

"You think it's a secret?" Michelle asked. "Everyone knows you're stalking him. He's even shut off his cell phone so he won't receive—" She clapped her hand over her mouth. "Oops, I didn't mean to let that slip out."

"Yes, you did," Sudi spat back. "That's exactly

what you wanted to say. I bet you've been trying to figure out a way to fit that into the conversation."

"Don't waste your time being upset with me." Michelle tossed her hair. "You should be pissed at Scott. He's the one who dumped you."

Sudi inhaled sharply.

Michelle went on, "Why don't you forget about him and invite Raul over to your house?"

Sudi focused her gaze on Sara. "You told her about Raul?"

"Yes," Sara confessed unabashedly. "I mean, if Scott's just going to let things drift and not even bother to break up with you—"

"Is that what you think?" One glance at Sara told Sudi it was. "I can't believe you didn't tell me something that important."

"When have you had time for Sara so that she *could* even tell you?" Michelle asked. "You're always off with your other friends."

"That's not true," Sudi protested.

"Besides, Raul's the perfect stand-in, until you find someone new," Michelle went on. "Speak of the devil."

Sudi turned.

Raul was nearby, bouncing a soccer ball on his knee. He caught the ball on the top of his foot and balanced it there.

After a silence, Sara said, "He looks a lot like Scott. I hadn't noticed that before."

Sudi had, and she wondered, not for the first time, if Raul's resemblance to Scott—the scruffy hair, lean muscles, sweet baby face—was the reason she had been crushing on him. Maybe Michelle was right. Maybe he was a replacement.

Looking up, Raul caught all three girls staring at him. He lost his concentration and the ball bounced away from him. He gave an embarrassed smile before dashing into the street after the ball. He scooped it up and walked back to them. "Hey."

"Sudi was wondering if you wanted to go over to her house tonight," Michelle blurted out.

Sudi turned to Michelle, ready to strangle her.

"I'd like that," Raul said, smiling at Sudi.

Flustered, Sudi pulled a pen and paper from her purse. "Um, sure. Let me give you my address."

"I know where you live," he said, blushing a bit.

Sudi looked up, surprised. "You do?"

He nodded. "What time do you want me to come over?"

"Six," Michelle answered for Sudi.

Raul looked at Sudi to make sure.

"Six is great." Sudi nodded.

Raul glanced at his watch. "I'd better go." He waved good-bye, then kicked the ball and chased after it.

"Now you have a *real* reason for not going with us." Michelle grinned before sliding into the car.

"I'll call you tonight," Sara promised.

When the car drove away, unexpected tears came to Sudi's eyes. She and Sara had always been inseparable, but since Sudi had been summoned and forced to keep secrets from her best friend, they were quickly growing apart. And now Michelle was wedging herself between them.

Disheartened, Sudi brushed the tears away and started for home.

At the corner, a sudden gust lifted the leaves and blew them in a twisting pattern that drew her attention back to the school.

Zack stood at the entrance, watching her.

Alone on the street near her house, Sudi slowed her steps and peered into the shadows. A primitive instinct told her that she was in danger. Something was there in the dark with her.

Even though she was nervous, she didn't run. She waited. Soon, velvet darkness glided across the grass beneath the evergreens. The pine needles swished back and forth, releasing their fragrance into the night air.

As Sudi stepped closer to investigate, she

heard her sisters' screams coming from inside the house.

"Carrie! Nicole!" Sudi sprinted up the porch steps, fumbled with her key, unlocked the door, and flung herself inside. She skidded on something spilled on the floor and started to fall, but then caught herself on a side table.

Harsh incense smoke burned her throat and lungs.

Carrie was holding a bowl filled with the same grainy stuff that covered the floor.

"What are you doing?" Sudi asked, closing the front door. "The house is a mess."

Nicole ran down the stairs, an open box of kosher salt clutched in the crook of her arm.

Sudi's younger sisters were identical twins, but Nicole loved to eat, and too many second helpings had given her a plump shape, while Carrie's picky eating kept her very thin. They no longer wore the same size, but they still shared an unsettling way of looking at Sudi.

"It's your fault," Nicole said, close to tears, her face red and sweaty. "You did it."

"Did what?" Sudi took quick inventory. They

couldn't know about the geometry problems she had copied off Sara's homework. And even if they did, why would they care?

Sighing, Carrie sat on the bottom step and gathered her pale blond hair into a ponytail. "You brought a ghost into the house."

"A ghost?" Sudi repeated as pictures of the phantom shadow beneath the evergreens outside flashed through her mind. She quickly dismissed the idea. After all, a ghost was sheer, thin, and transparent, not solid and black. Besides, the dark shape that she had just seen was more likely her imagination working overtime than an apparition; if the shadow had actually been something dangerous, wouldn't it have attacked her?

Nicole plunked herself down next to Carrie. "I'm not living in a haunted house."

"Why do you think the house is haunted?" Sudi asked.

"Duh," Carrie said. "A ghost."

"We think you brought it into the house," Nicole added.

"Me?"

"You have a peculiar aura." Carrie studied

Sudi. "It's different from what everyone else has. That's most likely what attracted the ghost to you."

"Our Ouija board said the ghost traveled on a bracelet." Nicole licked the salt from her fingers. "It probably urged you to buy the bracelet you're wearing."

Sudi felt doubtful but held up her wrist.

Inlaid with turquoise, her gold bracelet reflected the light. She'd stolen it from the tomb in which she, Meri, and Dalila had been imprisoned when they'd traveled back in time to ancient Egypt. "How could a bracelet bring a ghost into the house?"

"It works like an anchor," Nicole said. "Spirits sometimes become attached to things."

A familiar gnawing started in Sudi's stomach. She worried about her sisters' interest in the occult. In kindergarten their teacher had told them that twins have a psychic connection to each other. And, misunderstanding the comment, the two of them had concluded that *they* had supernatural powers. Sudi used to tell them that such things didn't exist. Now she knew better.

"If you two understood all the scary things that are out there in the world, you wouldn't be so eager to play around with your Ouija board," Sudi said, without thinking. "I wish you'd just stop messing—"

"Whoa!" Nicole jumped up. "What made you a believer?"

Carrie joined Nicole. "You always told us you didn't believe in that kind of stuff. You called it nonsense. What happened?"

Sudi realized her mistake. "I'm just humoring you because I have a friend coming over and I need to get the house cleaned up fast."

"That's not even a good lie," Carrie said in a challenging tone.

"We're waiting," Nicole added, angling closer.

Soft thumping came from upstairs.

"The ghost," Nicole whispered.

Immediately, Sudi knew the reason her sisters thought the house was haunted. Abdel had been trying to teach her how to use her wand, and so far she hadn't been able to control it. At night it bumped around her room like an unruly dog. That morning she had left it tied to the leg of her desk, but it must have broken free during the day.

Panicked, Sudi raced up the stairs ahead of

Carrie. She threw herself in front of her bedroom door and spread her arms out, stopping her sisters from rushing inside.

"You have to let us into your room," Nicole said, her chest heaving as she tried to catch her breath.

"Sorry. Off limits." Sudi eased inside, closed and locked the door, ignoring her sisters' pleas. No way could she let them see what was hidden in her room.

Her yellow cat, Patty Pie, was keeping watch on something under the bed. The comforter billowed, and tiny jeweled eyes peeked out at Sudi. Pie jumped back and hissed, batting wildly at the wand with his paw.

"I can't believe you don't even know how to defend yourself against a cat," Sudi scolded her wand as she lifted Pie and set the cat on top of her desk. "It's safe now." She kept her voice low to avoid her sisters—who were most likely listening at the door—from hearing.

Hesitating at first, her wand finally rolled out. Made of bronze and less than a yard long, it looked like a walking stick with the head of a snake.

Sudi picked it up, then smoothed her fingers over the Egyptian hieroglyphs etched into the side. The beetles, frogs, and baboons carved into the surface squirmed beneath her touch. She ignored what the wand was trying to tell her and set it inside her closet. "Maybe you'll be quiet in here."

As she started to close the door, the wand whimpered.

"Don't tell me you're afraid of the dark," Sudi said.

When the wand didn't answer, she switched on the closet light and grumbled, "Just my luck."

Sudi glanced at the clock. Raul would be arriving soon. She had just five minutes for makeup, but she knew the drill. She defined her eyes with gray shadow from lash line to crease and then ran the pencil under her lower eyelid. Rolling on mascara, she wished she had time for false lashes. At last she swiped on lipstick and headed back downstairs.

Near the front door, her sisters were pulling on their coats.

Nicole wrapped a scarf around her neck, but she wasn't quick enough to hide the earrings she'd snatched from Sudi's jewelry box. She caught Sudi's accusing look. "You left them in the bathroom," she said.

"It's okay." Sudi tried to hug her sisters, but they squirmed away from her.

"We're going to the library." Carrie opened the door.

"Homework?" Sudi asked.

"Research on how to do an exorcism," Nicole said, pulling on her gloves.

"I wish you wouldn't . . ." Sudi let her words trail off and followed her sisters onto the porch.

She watched them head down the walk, then scanned the evergreens where the suspicious dark shape had been lurking before. Looking ordinary now, the same shape just shifted back and forth, not as a phantom, but as a shadow cast by a bough bending in the breeze.

Sudi called after her sisters. "Stay together," she yelled, not understanding her own uneasiness. They had walked to the library at night before. "Don't take too long!"

She left the front door open to get rid of the bitter smoke, then snuffed out the incense and took the plates to the kitchen. Minutes later, as she started vacuuming up the salt, cold fingers touched her arm. She jumped, catching a scream in her throat.

Raul switched off the vacuum cleaner. "I thought you left the front door open for me." He gave her a self-conscious grin. "I didn't mean to scare you."

"*You* didn't," Sudi lied, even though her heart was still running a marathon. "My sisters had been talking about—" She looked into his eyes. "Forget it. I don't want to talk about them." Desperate to change the subject she asked, "Do you tango?"

"Of course," he laughed. "I'm from Buenos Aires. We dance the tango in the streets." Then, humming a melody, he pulled her against him.

She squealed as Raul led her in an ankle-breaking series of steps. The pressure of his hand against her back let her know which way to move. She still messed up, but didn't really care. She loved the way he held her with such strength.

When at last he stopped, she said, "You're an incredible dancer."

"And I love your boldness." He kissed her hand.

Dizziness swept through her. "I'm starved,"

she said. "I haven't eaten all day." She led him into the kitchen, then carried the cookie jar over to the table and pulled out a half gallon of milk from the refrigerator.

After an hour of conversation and chocolate-chip cookies, Raul stopped talking and stared down at his empty glass. The silence meant only one thing to Sudi. He wanted to kiss her. She hooked a finger through the belt loop of his jeans, then closed her eyes, waiting.

He touched her face—the caress so gentle, she sighed. She lifted her free hand to hold his fingers against her cheek. But instead of touching his hand, she patted her own skin. Her eyes flashed open.

Raul was staring at her. He held a cookie, poised motionless halfway toward his mouth. "Do you have a toothache?"

"What?" she asked, feeling herself blush.

"You closed your eyes and touched your cheek. I thought maybe you were in pain," Raul explained.

But if he hadn't touched her, then who had?

"You're joking," she said. "You just touched me." Then another thought pushed all others aside. *Toothache?* Is that what guys saw on her face when they kissed her? Did she look like she was in pain?

The back door opened. Her sisters crept through the mud porch, whispering to each other. When they entered the kitchen, Sudi knew from their sheepish grins that they had been trying to sneak inside unheard.

Under her coat Nicole held a jar filled with water.

Sudi gasped. "You stole holy water from the church again, didn't you? Mom is going to—"

"How will she find out unless you tell her?" Carrie asked. "Besides, we left a donation."

"Holy water?" Raul looked puzzled. "Are you fighting a vampire?" he teased.

"They think the house is haunted," Sudi explained.

"What makes you think that?" Raul asked, looking at Sudi's sisters.

"Sheesh," Nicole said. "A ghost. Can't you feel its presence?"

"It's stronger than before," Carrie added. "We better hurry."

"Maybe you should be concerned about the spirit," Raul said gently. "Something might have happened to it and now it's trying to get your attention so you'll help it pass on to the other side."

Nicole looked at Carrie, then back at Raul. "You think the ghost has, like, deep emotional issues that went unresolved in life?"

Raul nodded good-naturedly.

"The ghost is toast," Nicole said. "We're getting rid of it."

Raul looked at Sudi. "I tried."

"Don't humor them." Sudi took Raul's hand. "Let's go into the living room."

But as they started to leave the kitchen, Carrie screamed, "There it is!" She grabbed the box of salt, dug her hand inside it, and threw a handful into the air.

Sudi ducked.

Raul wasn't as fast. "Ouch!"

"You got salt in his eyes," Sudi scolded; she turned to Raul. "There's a bathroom down here. You can wash out your eyes." She led him around the staircase, then ushered him inside the bathroom and turned on the faucet.

He pushed her out of the bathroom and closed the door.

"Why'd you do that?" Sudi asked, facing her sisters.

"It's creepy the way he looks so much like Scott," Carrie said, ignoring her question. "Are you sure you really like him? Maybe—"

Sudi clapped her hand over Carrie's mouth. "Yes, I like him, and don't change the subject. Why'd you throw salt on him? Besides, whoever heard of using salt on a ghost? Why couldn't you use something normal, like a crucifix?"

Nicole rolled her eyes. "Everyone knows ghosts aren't afraid of a cross. You've got them confused with vampires. Salt stops a ghost."

The bathroom door opened, and Raul stepped out, his eyes red. "Don't be mad at your sisters. A little salt can't hurt me."

"But obviously it has," Sudi said. "You can't stop blinking."

"I'm fine," he said, squinting. "But it's late. I should be going home."

Reluctantly, Sudi followed him to the door and walked outside into the cold winter air to say good-bye.

Side by side, leaning against each other, they

stared out at the night. Sudi wished she could think of a way to get him back inside. She didn't want the evening to end, not like that anyway.

"Do you know the two guys in the car?" Raul asked, breaking the silence.

Sudi followed his gaze.

Under the streetlight, Brian's Cadillac idled next to the curb, white vapor spewing from the tailpipe. Brian and Scott sat in the front, watching Sudi through the windshield.

"No," she groaned. Michelle had set her up again.

Raul half turned and whispered into her ear, "It's okay. I knew you had a boyfriend."

Flustered, she glanced up at him. "You did?"

He seemed amused.

"But that doesn't make it right," she continued. "I should have . . . I didn't . . ."

"I know." His fingers stroked her back. "That makes me think you like me as much as I like you."

He didn't wait for her reply but skipped down the porch steps and walked past the Cadillac with a light, happy bounce in his stride.

Brian and Scott climbed out of the car. Scott

looked more handsome than Sudi remembered, but seeing him didn't make her happy, because even from a distance she could see the hurt in his eyes.

"Damn, Sudi," Brian called. "Aren't you ever going to get over me?"

"You?!" Sudi shouted back. "How is this about *you*?"

"Scott likes you," Brian said.

Scott didn't say a word, just stood there, his gorgeous eyes still watching Sudi.

"You should be satisfied with him," Brian continued, "but you keep playing the field, hoping you'll find someone just like me."

"That is so not true," she said.

Her sisters ran out on the porch and stood beside her.

"Here's a clue, Sudi," Brian said in his own inimitable way. "No matter how many other guys you date, you'll never find another one like me."

"I hope not!" Carrie fired back.

"Why would I ever want to date another you?" Sudi said, her voice starting to tremble.

"Then what is this about, Sudi?" Scott asked. For a moment, she thought he was going to say something more, but then he climbed back into the car.

Brian got in behind the steering wheel and gunned the engine.

When the Cadillac sped away, Sudi followed her sisters back inside. She couldn't believe how easily she'd been manipulated by Michelle. More than anything she wanted revenge, but right now she had a bigger problem. How could she like two guys at the same time?

CHAPTER 3

The next afternoon, a loud thump came from Sudi's closet. She had taped her wand on the closet wall behind her clothes the night before so it couldn't bump around her room and keep her awake but, judging by the noise it was making now, the wand was frantically trying to break free. Sudi didn't get up to investigate. Instead, she hugged her pillow and sprawled out on her bed, trying to think of an excuse to avoid going over to Abdel's.

She had stayed home from school, faking the

flu, telling her mother she didn't feel well, which was now true. But it was her own fault—earlier that afternoon, when Mrs. Finders, the house-keeper, had started baking, Sudi had snuck into the kitchen and stolen a big hunk of chocolate-chip cookie dough.

Unexpectedly, her bedroom door flew open, and Sara stepped in.

"I knew you weren't really sick!" Sara squealed. "You should have called me. I would have cut classes and spent the day with you." She threw her coat and scarf over the desk chair, then sat on the edge of the bed and started taking off her black boots with the buckles and studs.

Sudi anxiously listened. The wand was—thankfully—being quiet.

"Give me the report," Sudi said, pulling the sleeves of her sweater down over her hands so she wouldn't nervously chew on her fingernails.

"Brian told everyone how he and Scott caught you with Raul," Sara said excitedly. "Brian says that both guys are madly in love with you."

"Really?" Sudi asked, surprised. "I thought they'd both hate me."

"You're such a heartbreaker." Sara crawled on the bed and snatched the bowl of cookie dough away from her. "So, which one do you like?"

"That's the problem," Sudi answered, falling back against her pillows. "I like them both. How can I like two guys at the same time? That's just—"

"You," Sara laughed. "You've always liked more than one guy, except for the time you were with Brian."

Sudi rolled her eyes. "Why does every conversation always turn back to Brian?"

"Stop complaining." Sara scooped up some more cookie dough. "Most girls would give a year's allowance to have your problems."

Sudi's phone beeped.

Leaning over, Sara read the one-word text message. "*Hurry.* Is that a code for meeting Raul or Scott?" she asked, licking her fingers. "You're going to be a legend. Who are you meeting?"

"I was supposed to go over to Abdel's," Sudi said, "and I'm already late."

The excitement drained from Sara's face. Her smile didn't conceal her disappointment. She set the bowl aside and scooted off the bed.

"That's okay," she said, grabbing her boots. "I needed to go home and get started on my homework anyway."

While Sara pulled on her boots, Sudi stepped into the closet. As quietly as she could, she pushed her clothes aside, then ripped away the masking tape that held the wand in place. It fell off the wall, bucked, and tried to roll away from her. Sudi caught it and stuffed it into an old sports bag she used for carrying baseball equipment down to the park. Then, lifting the strap over her shoulder, she turned.

Sara was watching her. "What's with the walking stick?" Sara asked. "I mean, you had it taped to your wall, and now you've put it in a bag. Are you taking it with you?"

Sudi bit her lip, unable to come up with a lie to explain what she had just done. Stalling, she stepped into her sneakers.

Sara frowned and continued, "You know it's not just me who's noticing how . . ."

". . . Weird I've been acting?" Sudi asked.

"I'm sorry, but yeah," Sara said. "Leo told everyone that you thought some guy dressed in black was following you around school."

"But someone was," Sudi started, then stopped, when she realized how ridiculous she sounded.

"Kids are saying that since your breakup with Brian—"

"The way I'm acting has nothing to do with Brian," Sudi snapped back.

"Then, what is it?" Sara asked.

Sudi brushed past her. "If I told you, you wouldn't believe me anyway."

"Try me," Sara said. "You used to tell me everything."

"That was before—" Sudi hesitated.

Fortunately, the cell phone beeped again at that moment.

Sudi glanced at the new message. "I have to go," she said and headed out into the hallway. "I'll call you tonight."

Sara raced after her. "I've got a rock in my stomach, Sudi. That really scary feeling like we used to get when we were doing something risky. Only this time, that rock is as big as a boulder, because I'm so worried about you. Please, tell me what's going on."

Sudi walked down the stairs in silence, trying

to think of a way to explain things to Sara. "I'm afraid," she admitted when they reached the bottom step.

"Of what?" Sara asked. "Did Brian . . . ?"

"Not Brian." Sudi took her black leather bomber jacket off the hook by the door and pulled it on. "My life's been ripped apart," she confessed. "I'll call you tonight and tell you everything."

"Promise?" Sara asked as they stepped out on the porch together.

"I promise," Sudi said.

They hooked little fingers the way they had done when they were in elementary school, only now neither was able to smile. They faced each other with a desperate kind of sadness, each trying to hold on to what their friendship had been.

Then, clutching the sports bag tight against her chest so Sara couldn't see the way the wand was wiggling inside, Sudi said, "You're not going to believe anything I tell you anyway."

Without waiting for her reply, Sudi sprinted down the street.

CHAPTER 4

Half an hour later, Sudi entered the yellow row house in Georgetown where Abdel lived. Ancient magic rushed around her, spells of protection cast by Descendants who had lived and died before she was born. Then, satisfied that she was not an intruder, the magic left her standing alone in the dark again.

Her throat tightened with the anger that rose to cover her helplessness. She didn't want to be there. She should have been at home eating cookie dough and hanging out with Sara.

"Why me?" she whispered.

"The sacred birthmark is a blessing," a voice said, startling her.

She jumped and looked around. She wondered if the voice had come from her wand, but Abdel had never told her that it could speak.

"You're foolish not to feel proud that you were chosen," the voice added.

"That's all I need," Sudi grumbled. "You don't obey me, and now you're scolding me?"

When the wand didn't answer, Sudi turned off her cell phone, picked up the sports bag, and started up the stairs; the old wood creaked under her weight.

In the doorway to a small room on the third floor, she paused. Flames burned from wicks set inside oil-filled clay bowls. The flickering light reflected off the copper chests in which the secrets of the gods in the Book of Thoth, written by *Djehuti*, were kept.

Meri and Dalila were already there, sitting at a round table studying an unrolled papyrus.

In the firelight, Dalila looked breathtakingly beautiful. She was wearing the belted orange sweater that Sudi had picked out for her. She glanced up, seeming to sense Sudi watching her.

"Sudi?" she asked, rising. "Are you all right?"

"I heard what Michelle did to you," Meri said, jumping up. She was still dressed in her school uniform from Entre Nous Academy, the private school she attended with Scott and Michelle—the standard gray skirt, blue blazer, and white shirt and socks—but covering her legs were black fishnet hose.

Meri's mother was the senior senator from California. Political analysts said that she was going to win her party's presidential nomination, but, for Meri's sake, Sudi hoped that the senator didn't succeed. Meri already had photographers chasing after her, and if her mother became the next president, it would only get worse

"Michelle acted so innocent at school today," Meri said. "She told me it was just a coincidence that Scott went over to your house while Raul was there."

"She's a fool if she thinks we'll believe that," Dalila said, pulling Sudi to the table. "I don't need to cast a spell to know that Michelle's behind this."

She poured tea into a cup and handed it to Sudi. A spicy fragrance filled the air.

"Scott is so miserable," Meri added. "I know he still likes you."

While Sudi sipped the hot tea, Dalila asked, "Have you seen Carter?"

Sudi shook her head. "No one has seen him for a couple of weeks." Secretly, Sudi worried that he was in trouble.

Dalila touched the gold bracelet that Carter had given her. She had been forced to leave it in ancient Egypt the last time the girls were there, in the very tomb that her uncle was now excavating.

"My uncle just brought the bracelet back to me," Dalila explained. "I'm going to take that as a good sign. If it can survive for four thousand years and find its way back to me, then maybe Carter will find a way back to me, too."

Meri and Sudi exchanged quick glances. Dalila's heartache was obvious.

"I'm sure he'll come back soon," Sudi offered, even though his absence baffled her.

"Maybe his dad or mom got transfers and you'll get a letter from him any day," Meri added.

Dalila smiled, grateful for their sympathy.

"Why didn't either of you bring your wands with you?" Sudi asked, changing the subject.

"Abdel just wants to talk to us tonight," Meri said. "We'll train our wands tomorrow."

"Another session," Sudi groaned. "Since we've learned the truth about his past, he's been running our training like boot camp."

Abdel hadn't wanted to start their real instruction until they knew that he had been a tomb robber during the time of the pharaohs.

"He's making up for lost time," Dalila agreed. "He's given us a rigorous schedule."

"Be quiet," Meri warned. Feline ears poked out of her hair and twitched, listening for something.

Transformation was just one of the gifts that they had been given when they were summoned. Meri could turn into a cat. Dalila became a fire-breathing cobra, and Sudi transformed into a bird.

"Abdel's coming," Meri whispered. "And by the way he's muttering to himself, I know he's upset." Her ears slid back down and disappeared.

Immediately, the attic door scraped open.

"I'm worried," Dalila whispered. "My uncle has been very distraught, too." Her uncle was the famous Egyptologist Anwar Serenptah. Her own parents had been killed in a cave-in while excavating a tomb in the Valley of the Kings, when Dalila was seven years old. Since that time she had lived with her uncle.

All three girls watched the door as the sound of approaching footsteps filled the stairwell. Moments later, Abdel entered the room, his face haggard, his dark, scruffy hair hanging in his eyes.

When Sudi had first met him, she had assumed that he was Scott's friend. He had the Entre Nous look: a three-hundred-dollar haircut and outrageously expensive clothes. Sudi wondered where he got his money. He didn't have a job, but he had to have some source of income. Her mind flashed to the treasures that he had robbed from the tombs. Was it possible that he still had some priceless artifacts hidden away?

"Something in the present is affecting the past," Abdel said solemnly as he joined them.

Baffled, Sudi asked, "How could something in the present affect the past?"

"You mean, like, changing history?" Meri asked. "How could you even know if that were happening?"

Abdel held Meri's gaze. He had fallen deeply in love with her long ago in ancient Egypt. She was the reason he had become an Hour priest.

"I'm certain that someone from the past has discovered a way to enter the present," Abdel said. "And whoever it is has found immense power here, because the constellation Sahu, the home of Osiris, is changing position and pulling other stars closer to it. This reveals how cataclysmic the change in the past will be. If successful, the future, as well as our own time, will cease to exist, because the world will have been destroyed centuries before."

Dalila looked worried. "My uncle saw something, too. He called it a cosmic disaster."

"What if the stars collapse and form a black hole?" Meri asked. "Would the earth be sucked into it, too?"

"It could be a way to return the universe to the chaos from which it came," Abdel answered.

"If something that major were going to happen," Sudi said, "scientists would know about it. It would be headlining the news."

Abdel considered this. "Possibly, but what they saw wouldn't fit into any of their current theories. They wouldn't make an announcement until they found a rational explanation."

Meri spoke, a strange look on her face. "My mom is on the Senate Intelligence Committee. She can't tell me what's going on, but twice this week agents have come to our house late at night and taken my mother someplace. Do you think they have an idea of what's going on?"

Sudi felt a chill rush through her. She looked at Abdel.

"Very possible." He nodded. "I'm confident that the Cult of Anubis is behind this plan, but I am even more confident that the three of you will find a way to stop it before anything disastrous happens."

"But how?" Dalila asked. "What are we supposed to do?"

"You are the Enchantress," Abdel said. "You should be able to see more than I can. Haven't you been looking at the night sky?"

"I only see stars," she whispered, ashamed.

Dalila was descended from people who possessed

supernatural powers. Her ancestors were the ones who had tamed the fiery spirits that had existed before creation. Her mother had been called Rekhet, a word that meant "knowing one," and Dalila had inherited her magic.

Sudi placed an arm around Dalila to comfort her.

"First, you must discover the source of the power," Abdel said. But as he continued talking on and on about the pattern of the stars, Sudi drifted off, daydreaming. She thought of the night sky, and then couldn't help thinking about how romantic it would be on a clear, starry night with Raul. . . . She imagined kissing him, and then she thought about Scott, and about kissing him. She considered her situation. Guys had two girlfriends all the time, keeping one secret from the other. She wondered if she dared. A guy who ran around was cool, but a girl who did the same quickly earned a bad reputation.

Meri nudged Sudi, rousing her from her thoughts.

Abdel had been talking to her. "I was explaining why you shouldn't keep your wand in the sports bag," Abdel said.

Slowly, Sudi became aware of the soft thumping. She glanced down. Her wand had pushed the zipper back and was struggling to get out.

"How will you know if it's trying to warn you of danger?" Abdel asked.

"Right now it *is* my biggest danger." Sudi rolled up her sweater sleeve and stretched out her arm so they could see her bruises. "My wand did this. Besides, I don't think it's going to be much help if I do get in trouble, because it's afraid of my cat and even the dark."

Abdel studied Sudi in a way that made her uncomfortable. "It's interesting that of all the wands this is the one that has been given to you."

"It's started talking to me," she said. "And it doesn't have a very pleasing personality."

"I've never heard of a wand talking to its master." Abdel seemed skeptical.

"This one does," Sudi argued. "It scolds me."

All three stared at her.

"I'm not feeling very well," Sudi said abruptly, wishing she hadn't brought it up. Suddenly she just wanted to get out of there. To go hang out with her friends. She thought about Nana and Emily, her old dance crew. How long had it been since she'd seen them? Maybe there was still time to call Sara and see if she wanted to find a party.

"I'll cast a spell to make you feel better," Dalila offered.

"No!" Sudi's hand shot up to shield her face. "Just let me go home and be miserable. Sometimes it's good to feel bad."

"I'll have my driver give you a ride home," Meri said, but when she started to get up, Abdel stopped her.

"Let her go," he said quietly.

Sudi picked up the sports bag and hurried from the room. She knew Abdel had sensed her lie, so why had he let her leave so easily? On other nights he made her stay until her mouth felt dry and her back ached from casting spells.

At the front door she put on her coat. When she stepped outside, the winter cold stung her face. Through the tangled canopy of branches, she gazed up at the starry night and wondered what Abdel and Dalila's uncle saw when they studied the heavens. She saw only the moon and stars.

Deep in concentration, she didn't notice the

odd way the wind twisted through the trees. Branches bent low, as if holding a heavy weight, before snapping back into place.

Near her house an icy stream of air caressed her face. The fine hair on the back of her neck rose in response, and, with terrible clarity, she knew she was no longer alone.

CHAPTER 5

"I was just coming over to your house," a familiar voice said.

"Raul?" Sudi did a quick about-face and strolled back to him.

In the moonlight, he looked impossibly handsome, his eyes almost shimmering. "There's a big party tonight, and I was hoping you'd go with me." He wrapped his arms, warm and strong, around her. "I tried to call you on your cell phone, but you didn't answer."

"I had to turn it off." She leaned against him, loving the feel of his body, his scent of musk and soap.

Her wand bucked wildly, banging the sports bag against her side, but Raul didn't seem to notice. She tightened her grip on the canvas bag and prayed the wand wouldn't speak.

"Do you want to go with me?" he asked.

"More than anything." She pulled back so she could see his face. "But my parents won't let me go out on school nights."

"Is that your way of telling me *no* without hurting my feelings?" he asked. "I wouldn't be here if I hadn't heard that you've gone out on a school night before."

"That's true." She wondered what he'd heard and from whom. "But I didn't have permission." She wasn't going to tell Raul about the times she had snuck out to meet Brian.

Besides, since the tree outside her bedroom had been trimmed back, the jump from her window to the branch below the sill felt too risky, even for a night with Raul. Then another idea came to her. Maybe she could get out after all.

"Wait for me around the corner." She started toward her house. "I'll be there in twenty minutes."

"What are you going to tell your parents?" he asked anxiously.

"I'm not going to tell them anything," she replied.

But instead of looking intrigued, he seemed even more nervous. "Maybe we should go out another time, then. This weekend maybe."

She had a sudden urge to kiss him. Besides being good-looking, he was shy and apprehensive, so different from the other guys she had dated. "Don't worry so much," she said.

"But how are you going to sneak out?" He stared at her house. "I don't want you to do anything unsafe."

She smiled to herself, delighted. She was dating a total goody-goody. She liked the idea of being the bad one in the relationship.

"Sudi," he said, interrupting her thoughts. "Tell me."

"I'm going to change into a bird and fly out," she said flippantly.

At last he nodded and even tried to laugh. "I'll be in my father's car."

She paused. "How will I know it?"

"It's a Maserati coupe," he said self-consciously.

Speechless, Sudi stared at him.

"What's wrong?" he asked.

She sighed. "A Maserati. That's my dream car." She headed toward her house. "Wait for me. I'll be there soon." Then she swung around and hurried up the porch steps.

The smell of stuffed peppers filled the house.

"Does anyone know where the aspirins are?" Sudi yelled, closing the front door behind her.

"What's wrong?" Mrs. Finders hurried from the kitchen, a pot holder in her hand.

"I think I have a relapse of the flu," Sudi lied, looking around the room. This was going to be a snap. Her parents weren't even home. "I'm going back to bed."

"I'll bring you some soup." Mrs. Finders headed into the kitchen.

Sudi put a hand to her stomach. "No, thank you. I'm a little nauseous. I'll just go on to bed."

When Mrs. Finders had safely disappeared, Sudi raced up the stairs.

Nicole stopped her halfway. "You are so not

sick. You spent the day eating cookie dough."

"You have to help us with an exorcism," Carrie said, joining her twin. "You're the reason our house is haunted in the first place."

"I'll help you tomorrow morning," Sudi said, dodging between them.

When she heard them scrambling after her, she raced into her room and shut the door. "I promise," she said as she turned the lock. "But right now, I'm sick, and I'm going to bed."

She dropped the sports bag, took off her coat, then wiggled out of her jeans and sweater and slipped into the strapless push-up bra and slinky party dress that she had been dying to wear. The red silk clung to her body. She pulled on her heels and buckled the straps around her ankles.

As she stepped over to the window, her room was filled with an eerie glow from a source of light behind her. She glanced over her shoulder. Her wand had managed to escape from the sports bag. Hieroglyphs streamed down its side.

Irritated, she seized the masking tape from her desk, then took the wand and carried both into her closet.

"I'm not going to let you mess up my night." She taped the wand to the wall behind her clothes.

Then, with rising excitement, she hurried across the room, and opened her window. The winter chill rushed around her, but she wasn't about to ruin her outfit with a coat. Raul could keep her warm.

She leaned out into the night and stared up at the sky.

"Amun-Re," she whispered.

As she lifted her hands to the milky moon, a different kind of chill rushed through her, and for a moment she hesitated, wondering if it was sacrilegious to use the incantation so she could party. She looked up at the ring that the goddess Isis had given her. The gold band sparkled in the moonlight. Then, she remembered: Isis was practically the original party girl.

Reassured, she continued the incantation: "Eldest of the gods in the eastern sky, mysterious power of wind, make a path for me to change my earthly *khat* into that of beloved Bennu. *Xu kua.* I am glorious. *User Kua.* I am mighty. *Neteri kua.* I am strong."

A fierce pain burned through her, stronger than she remembered. Gripping the windowsill, she bent over. Her muscles cramped. A feverish ache rushed through her bones. She waited, unable to breathe. Finally, tiny feathers sprouted from her arms and grew into lush plumage. Her eyes moved to either side of her head. Each saw separately now, with the monocular vision of a bird. While her lips grew into a long beak, she stretched her wings.

When the change was complete, she flew out her window. Her avian instincts, strong on this night, urged her to fly over to the Potomac River. Instead, she glided up in circles toward the moon, then down, the wind holding her, and landed beneath the trees. Spontaneously she released a raucous cry of joy. Her screech echoed through the dark as she transformed back into a girl. She wondered how many neighbors had been startled away from their television sets to investigate the sound.

At last she stepped from the shadows and strode toward Raul, taking pleasure in the effect she was having on him

"Do you like my dress?" she teased, knowing he was looking at what the dress revealed.

He hurriedly took off his coat and draped it over her shoulders, then kissed her ear and whispered, "You're beautiful."

Still holding on to her waist, he opened the passenger-side door and helped her in.

She gave him her best sultry look and slid her legs into the car, letting her dress rise up to show them off. She was determined to have her kiss tonight.

The soft, deep hum of the engine vibrated through her as the car rumbled away from the curb. Excited to be riding in her dream car, she ran her fingers over the dashboard. The chalky feel surprised her. She glanced down at the pads of her fingers, and saw what looked like dust. Maybe his father didn't use the car that often.

She started to ask Raul about it, but instead decided to lean back and enjoy the ride.

Minutes later, when the car turned off U Street, she gasped, "You're taking me to an outlaw club."

He braked the car. "We can go somewhere else if you don't want to go there. I thought you'd like it."

"It's just a crazy coincidence," she explained,

"because earlier this evening, I had been thinking about going dancing." She playfully poked him. "Hurry. I can't wait."

He sped forward and quickly found a place to park.

She got out of the car and gave Raul back his coat.

"You'll freeze," he warned.

She cuddled against him. "You'll keep me warm." She smiled.

She could sense the party spirit even before they walked around the corner. Kids had spilled outside, in spite of the cold. Some danced and kissed, while others leaned against the cars parked illegally in the middle of the street and drank beers wrapped in brown paper bags.

During the day, the club looked like an abandoned and dilapidated building. *For Sale* signs in the windows and graffiti across the bricks gave no clue that a dance club claimed the space at night. Now, three generators buzzed on the sidewalk, giving energy to the garish lights. The music coming from inside was loud. The splintered porch railing shook with the beat.

At the entrance, T.J., the largest of the security guards, stopped Raul. "Get back in line," he ordered. His massive muscles strained against his black shirt.

"You're not going to let us through?" Sudi asked. "I've never been stopped before."

Sudden recognition flashed across T.J.'s face. "Sudi, where have you been?" He pulled her forward and squeezed her against his huge body. "Get on inside. It's cold out here." He waved them through.

"What kind of spell did you cast over him?" Raul teased. "He didn't even bother to frisk me."

"Bouncers always let the cute girls in," she answered and tossed him a look.

"Then that's just another reason I'm glad to be with you," Raul said.

She took his hand and guided him inside, heading toward the back, where she used to dance with Nana and Emily. When she neared the stage, the band stopped playing. The singer leaned in toward the microphone.

"Sudi's in the house tonight," he announced and gave her a wink.

Excitement rose inside her as kids turned and began shouting out her name.

Raul pulled her closer to him. "I didn't know you were so popular."

"With this crowd, I am," she said, beaming. "They love to watch me dance."

Nana and Emily pushed toward her, sweat glistening on their foreheads. Sudi squealed and hugged each one in turn.

The music started again, and then, side by side, the girls whooped and began dancing. Sudi loved the feel of the music, so loud it pounded through her. She began to relax and to realize how tense she had become worrying about her duties as a Descendant. She felt safe here, vamping it for the guys.

"You still have the killer moves," Emily said between songs.

"She's really improved since I gave her lessons," another voice said.

"Huh?" Sudi wheeled around.

Michelle, wearing a bikini top under her low-cut dress, bounced into Sudi, trying to mimic her moves.

Emily giggled and adjusted her studded hip belt.

"You're tripping if you think you can dance like Sudi," Nana said.

Michelle looked stunned. Then her mouth tightened and stretched into an ugly smile. "Sudi didn't know how to dance until I taught her. Tell them, Sudi."

Sudi gawked at Michelle. "Are you talking about fifth grade?"

Michelle glowered. "I gave you your start. If it weren't for me, you—"

"I get this dance." Raul took Sudi into his arms and rescued her from Michelle.

"Thank you," Sudi said.

He nuzzled her neck. "I don't want to share you with anyone tonight."

Wanting his kiss, Sudi moved her mouth toward his, but when she did, he pulled back.

"What's wrong?" she asked, surprised.

Without answering her question, he brushed his hand over the side of her face.

"You're acting like this is your first kiss," she teased and then suddenly she realized that it was. "I can't believe it. Someone as good-looking as you, and you've never kissed a girl before?"

"Don't say it so loudly," he said, looking around.

Impulsively, she brought his face down to hers and kissed him gently, with a butterfly's touch.

But instead of smiling back at her, he looked at his watch.

"Was it that awful?" she asked. "I thought you'd want more."

"We better leave now," he said, taking her hand.

"But we just got here." She didn't want to go home and spend a miserable night wondering why he didn't want to kiss her. "Stay with me. I love to dance."

He glanced down at his watch again. "I can't. I have to go."

She studied him as other thoughts raced through her mind. Maybe he wanted more than his first kiss. "I'm not . . . I don't . . ." she stuttered.

On the other hand, it could have been just that he was incredibly shy and too embarrassed to kiss in public. Whatever his reason, she wasn't going to let him bust her fun. "I'll catch a ride home with someone else," she said.

He looked concerned and then frowned. "I brought you here, so I should take you home."

She shook her head. "I'm staying." She edged back through the crowd to Emily and Nana.

Michelle was trying to dance with them, but her moves were stiff. Sudi joined them and playfully bumped Michelle with her hip.

But the friendly gesture only angered Michelle. "You made me lose the beat," she complained.

Emily raised an eyebrow. Both she and Nana eased away from Michelle. As they started dancing with Sudi, someone hugged her from behind. Confident that Raul had changed his mind and come back, Sudi smiled and turned.

Her smile faded away when she looked up and discovered that Brian was holding her. He squeezed her body against his.

"What are you doing?" Sudi asked, trying to push him away. "You hate me, remember?"

He didn't answer, but stared out at the dancers, seemingly unaware that he was even holding her. She stopped struggling, alert now, and apprehensive. The goddess Isis sometimes entranced Brian and used him to help the Descendants, and at the moment he definitely appeared dazed.

Then, using Brian's body as a screen, Sudi looked around the room. Her stomach dropped. Zack was wandering through the crowd not far from her. He glanced up and caught her eye. She stared back at him, too stunned to move, even when he slammed between the couple dancing next to him and pushed his way toward her.

With a surge of fear that sent adrenaline rushing through her, she tore free from Brian and backed up behind Nana and Emily.

"What's wrong?" Nana stopped dancing and put an arm around Sudi.

"Zack," Sudi replied.

"What's with him?" Emily asked. "Man, is he on something?"

Zack pushed Nana aside and reached for Sudi, his gaze deadly serious. His touch sent a strange shiver through her. She winced. He'd changed colognes, and the scent he was wearing stung the back of her nose. But there was something else—the Mephistophelian threat in his eyes; he wanted her soul.

She elbowed Zack and broke free, then lunged

into the crowd. Keeping her head down, she raced to the back exit.

Thirty kids, maybe more, loitered in front of the door, packed in tight, drinking, smoking, blocking her way out.

She raced back the way she'd come, burst through a line of girls rocking with the beat, charged down a narrow hallway, then turned again and found herself in total darkness.

The walls reverberated with the music, and the thunder of the drums rolled through her as she stretched out her hands and continued forward, her fingers tracing over the exposed laths. Her feet kicked against fallen plaster and broken glass. She had gone only a short distance when her survival instinct kicked in. The dank, stale-smelling hallway might lead to a basement staircase, Sudi reasoned, but it would be one she would never see until she was plummeting painfully down it. She had no choice, she had to go back.

She retraced her steps, then cautiously peered out into the adjoining hallway.

But when she started forward again, someone grabbed her shoulders and yanked her back.

${B}$rian swept Sudi into his arms and cradled her protectively against his chest.

"You're safe now," he said as he forced a path through the dancers on the main floor toward the front door.

Sudi took in a deep breath, grateful that he was the first person she'd run into. But then she saw the way some of the clubbers had stopped dancing and were looking at them. Even Nana and Emily were staring.

"Great," Sudi muttered. She had gotten rid of one problem only to gain a new one. Everyone who saw her with Brian was going to assume that they had gotten back together. Brian even looked bewitched, wearing a dreamy, love-struck expression.

Still carrying Sudi, Brian walked outside, past the security guard, around the line of buzzing generators.

"You can put me down now." She tried to squirm out of his arms. "I'll catch a cab."

"It's not safe yet." Brian tightened his grip, and, for a moment, his tenderness seemed real. Sudi glanced over his shoulder and saw the reason for his caution.

Zack had followed them outside. He stopped at the curb, the exhaust from the generators flapping his shirt. Michelle stood next to him. She hooked her arm through his, her gaze fierce.

"I think he's finished for tonight." Brian started down a side street.

This time Zack didn't trail after them. Michelle was talking to him, and even from this distance, Sudi knew she was peeved.

When they reached the Cadillac, Brian robotically opened the door and dropped Sudi onto the passenger seat. He pulled the seat belt across her body and buckled her in. With lumbering steps, he walked to the driver's side, got in, and stared at the steering wheel, seemingly confused.

"Can you drive?" Sudi asked.

"Of course I can." He turned the key in the ignition.

The engine rattled, rocking the car. The Cadillac lurched forward and zigzagged across the centerline.

"Original party girl?" Brian said with a disdainful huff. "Is that what you think of me?"

"Isis?" Sudi whipped her head around, expecting to see Isis staring back at her through Brian's eyes.

"I am the queen of magic," Brian said indignantly. "My power is above all others."

"I'm sorry if my thought offended you," Sudi added. "I didn't mean to be disrespectful. I was just unsure about using the incantation. I admire . . ." She let her words trail off. Why was she apologizing? If Isis was angry with her, what was she going to do, tell Sudi she couldn't be a Descendant anymore? That was exactly what Sudi wanted, anyway.

They rode in silence down the empty streets until Brian, still channeling the goddess, parked the car in the shadows near Sudi's house. He turned off the engine.

When Sudi started to open the car door, Brian clamped his hand around her wrist. "You're too jittery to change into a bird, and you won't remember the incantation anyway. You'll need to find another way inside."

Sudi didn't argue but waited to see what he would do next.

Brian climbed out of the car and headed to the backyard. He disappeared into the evergreens without waiting for Sudi to catch up.

Moments later, she found him near the house, staring down at the ground.

"That basement window looks open," he said when she reached him.

Hidden behind some bushes, the window had probably been left ajar since the summer. He nudged the dirty glass pane with the tip of his shoe.

"The ground is wet, so this should be easy."

He squatted down in front of the window and pried it all the way open, then glanced up at Sudi. "Climb in."

"No way," she said. "I don't even like going down into the basement when the lights are on. It's got spiders and all kinds of creepy bugs."

"Just do it," Brian snapped. "I want to get home and go to bed."

She studied him, wondering if the trance was wearing off. "All right," she said at last, "but I'm going to ruin my new dress."

Reluctantly, she bent down beside him, brushed the cobwebs aside, then sat on the cold ground and took off her shoes. She eased her feet into the opening and turned over onto her stomach. His hands guided her as she pushed herself backward. Her dress rode up, and slimy mud squished under her thighs and belly.

"Nice butt," Brian said.

She glanced up. For a second he had definitely snapped out of the trance; then his eyes widened and the vacant stare returned.

When she was ready to jump, he said, "Wait."

"What now?" she asked, barely able to hold on. Her legs were dangling heavily in the darkness below her, and her hands were slipping in the mud.

He leaned closer and said, "Matter is nothing more than a manifestation of energy."

Thanks for sharing that, she wanted to say, but thought better of it and let go.

She tumbled down and landed with a loud clatter on the boxes of Christmas-tree decorations that her mother had carefully packed away. The ornaments clinked and jingled, breaking beneath her weight.

After a moment, she rolled over and shakily stood up.

Covered with cobwebs and smelling like a grave, she limped up the basement stairs into the kitchen and then quietly crept up another flight of stairs to the bathroom, where she pulled off her dress and underwear and slipped them into the bottom of the hamper.

After that she took a long hot shower, using Nicole's peach-scented gel.

In her bedroom, still dripping wet, she closed the window, threw her towel aside, and pulled on her old sweats. She fell across her bed, depleted, and let self-pity and exhaustion overwhelm her.

Her wand had broken free from its masking-tape binding in the closet. It clunked toward her, its eerie orange glow lighting the room.

"Leave me alone and let me be miserable." She nudged its creepy snake's head away from the bed with her foot. "I hate being a Descendant, always waiting for the next demon to attack."

A sickening feeling came over her as she realized that her onetime friend Zack was the demon this time.

"You shouldn't feel so unhappy." The same voice that had scolded her at Abdel's house was trying to comfort her now.

"Shut up," Sudi said gruffly. "The last thing I want is advice from you." She picked up her pillow, and when she rolled over to throw it at her wand, her nose brushed through the pale, translucent face of a ghost.

CHAPTER 7

Sudi sat bolt upright, breathing fast. Her thoughts raced. *Calm down. Calm down. Whatever you do, don't wake up your parents.*

She jumped out of bed and lunged past the ghost.

In the hallway, the apparition streamed in front of her. Sudi ducked under it, aiming for her sisters' open doorway, and accidentally rammed her head into the wall.

"*Oooh,*" she moaned as she fell to the floor.

She got up, scrambed over the line of salt that was intended to ward off ghosts, and slammed into her sisters' room. Then she closed the door and switched on the overhead light, safe at last.

Catching her breath, she turned.

The ghost wavered beside her.

"No!" Sudi gasped.

Carrie sat up, startled, and nudged Nicole. "Sudi's met the ghost."

Wide awake now, Nicole threw back her covers, jumped out of bed, and rushed to her desk. She grabbed three green ribbons. Nine hazelnuts were glued to each one.

She handed a ribbon to Sudi. "Put it on."

Shakily, Sudi tied it around her neck.

Immediately, the ghost flitted away from her.

"What scared it?" she asked.

"Hazelnuts have been used for protection since ancient times," Carrie explained, tying back her hair with one of the ribbons.

Nicole struck a match and lit some sage incense, then waved it around the room before setting it on a tin plate.

The ghost floated away from the rising smoke

and hovered unhappily against the ceiling.

"Hurry," Nicole urged as she placed pillows at the bottom of the bedroom door so the smell couldn't escape and wake their parents.

Carrie lugged a large convex mirror from the closet. "We didn't steal it from a parking lot," she said, answering Sudi's look. "We bought it at an auto-supply store."

"Sit here," Nicole instructed, guiding Sudi to the center of the carpet.

Still trembling, Sudi sat down and watched Carrie adjust the mirror on a chair until it was at eye level with Sudi.

"Don't look in it," Nicole warned. "It's so the ghost will see itself and be frightened away."

Carrie and Nicole joined Sudi and clasped her hands, forming a circle of three. Then her sisters closed their eyes and began reciting words that Sudi didn't understand.

Unaffected, the ghost darted back to Sudi. "Have I done anything to harm you that you would treat me this way, making me ill with hazelnuts and the smoke from sage?" the ghost asked plaintively.

Afraid to look at the apparition, Sudi kept

her eyes down and shook her head.

The ghost continued, "If you would let me, I could bring the world to you, and yet you want to banish me."

"Don't listen to her," Nicole hissed.

The ghost fluttered closer to Sudi. "Would you not listen to me and make up your own mind? Your sisters are jealous, because I offer my services to you and not to them. That is the only reason they want to do this exorcism."

Carrie squeezed Sudi's hand. "Please, concentrate on what we're doing."

"I will be your humble and devoted servant," the ghost promised. "Imagine what I can do for you. Your mother wouldn't buy you the designer purse that you fell in love with, but I could go to Neiman Marcus right now and bring the object of your desire back to you. Would that please you, mistress?"

Tempted, Sudi thought of the delicate feel of the crinkly leather, then caught herself. "I can't have you steal for me," Sudi said. "That's wrong." But other possibilities were pushing their way into her mind.

Her sisters began speaking more rapidly, their eyes closed tight in concentration.

"I could spy for you," the ghost whispered urgently. "I could visit Scott and find out why he isn't returning your calls."

"You know about Scott, too?" Sudi turned and, for the first time, really looked at the ghost, with her pleasing smile, gentle eyes, and long flowing hair, which spun out around her head in a corona of curls. Sudi wondered what had happened to her and why she had died so young.

"I know everything about you," the ghost murmured. "I have been following you for many days, and I haven't harmed you, have I? So why are you letting your sisters send me away?"

Carrie yanked on Sudi's hand, pulling her attention back to the circle.

"Would I not be able to give you the revenge you desire?" the ghost asked, enticing her. "Imagine what I could do to your enemy, Michelle. She would never know you were the cause of her misfortune. I could protect you from other enemies as well."

With a ghost protecting her, Sudi wouldn't

have to worry about Zack. School could be a fun place again, like it had been before.

"Don't," Carrie groaned.

"Sorry." Sudi stood and pulled off the green ribbon. The hazelnuts tore free and bounced across the carpet.

"You are so going to regret this," Nicole warned.

CHAPTER 8

Feeling totally chic in her daringly short mini, Sudi strode down the hallway at school, exuding confidence. The ghost floated beside her, invisible but giggling excitedly, describing the way the guys were turning their heads to give Sudi a second look when she strolled by.

"Hey, vixen," Leo said, stepping around Sudi. "Glad to see you're back to being your old self again."

"I've missed *me*, too," Sudi said with a smile.

It felt so good to feel safe at school again. She would have given her ghost a great big smooch to show her gratitude, except that everyone around her would once again think she was losing her mind.

She opened her locker and glanced in the mirror. The ghost helped her comb out her hair; Sudi's curls rose and fell back down on her shoulders in perfect order. Eager to try out her ghost's protective powers on Zack, she had worn her neon-bright pink sweater so he'd be sure not to miss her.

When Sara's reflection appeared in the mirror behind Sudi, she turned, excited to see her friend. "I've been looking—"

"I heard you hooked up with Brian last night," Sara said, cutting her off. "I guess that's why you didn't call me."

The anger in her voice surprised Sudi. "Have you been crying?"

Sara's nose was swollen, her eyes red. "Would you care if I had?"

"Of course," Sudi answered. "What's wrong?"

Sara ignored the question. "Michelle said you let Brian carry you out to his car."

"That's what people saw," Sudi stammered, wondering why that would upset Sara enough to make her cry. "I was using him to leave the party, because another guy was bothering me."

"I heard about that, too," Sara said bitterly, and then she spat out the next words: "You knew I liked Zack."

Sudi froze.

"Michelle told me about the way you were teasing Zack and leading him on until he finally got tired of it and chased after you," Sara said, glowering. "I should have known. He was crazy about you in ninth grade, and I guess he never stopped liking you."

"That's not why he chased me," Sudi said. "And I didn't do anything to lead him on. I wouldn't do that to you."

"I've seen you dance, Sudi," Sara argued. "And just now I watched you flirt with Leo. What was that about? Do you have to have him, too?"

"I was just . . ."—Sudi searched for words— ". . . feeling good about myself."

"Is that what it's called?" Sara didn't wait for an answer. "If you were my friend, you would have discouraged Zack. He was my first real crush, Sudi."

"I like Scott and Raul, not Zack," Sudi said, defending herself. "I would never—"

"Yes, you would," Sara snapped. "You tried to warn me away from him. You wouldn't tell me why but now I guess I know. As soon as you found out that I liked him, you decided that you had to have him for yourself."

"That's not true," Sudi said.

"Isn't it? Michelle told me that the only reason you started liking Scott was because she liked him," Sara shot back. "You never told me that. I can't believe you stole him from her."

"You know that's not true," Sudi said. "How can you believe Michelle over me? We're best friends."

"If we're best friends, then why don't you ever ask me to go over to Abdel's house with you?" Sara asked, then hurried on to say, "Every time we plan to do something, you end up going over there instead, so you can hang out with Meri and Dalila."

"It's something I have to do, but I can't tell you the reason," Sudi said.

"Michelle says that it's because Meri's mom is

running for president," Sara said. "And you think that by being Meri's friend you can steal some of the spotlight for yourself. Michelle told me that everyone at Entre Nous thinks you're starstruck."

"Starstruck?" Sudi felt her anger rising. "Does that sound like me or Michelle?"

"A few weeks back, I would have said Michelle," Sara answered. "But now I don't know." She shook her head, then turned and walked away.

Sudi stared after her. They had had squabbles and petty quarrels before, always making up within minutes, but this argument was different. Sudi didn't know how they could go back to the way things had been before without telling Sara the truth.

By the time Sudi arrived at Abdel's house, her mood had sunk to its lowest ever, and even the sweet singing from her ghost didn't cheer her up.

Abdel opened the door and smiled. "We've been waiting for you."

Sudi marched inside, her anxiety rising. Dalila and Meri stood in the living room. Their wands, held like staffs, remained obediently at their sides.

"We were getting ready to come find you," Meri said. She wore frayed jeans, and her hair was slicked back in a ponytail that showed off her dangling earrings. "I thought maybe you'd forgotten about the lesson."

"Hurry and join us," Dalila said, looking glamorous in her chain-fringe necklace and low-cut top. "As soon as we're finished, we're going to that cute little café that I love and get macaroons and tea. My treat."

Dropping her sports bag, Sudi turned to Abdel. "Why are Meri and Dalila having such an easy time learning how to use their wands when I have to struggle so hard with mine?" She hated the whine in her voice. "I'm pathetic. Maybe you should give me another wand, one with training wheels."

Dalila regarded her with concern, but that only made Sudi feel worse.

"We'll help you," Meri offered.

"The wand can only be as good as its master," Abdel said calmly.

"If that was supposed to make me feel better, it didn't." Sudi tore off her coat, and as she was unwinding the three scarves from around her neck, Abdel continued, "No one blames the piano if the child can't play it. So why are you angry with your wand?"

"A piano doesn't hit back," Meri answered, defending Sudi. "Her arms are covered with bruises from her wand."

"You shouldn't be so hard on yourself, Sudi," Dalila said supportively. "Something is probably distracting you."

"Yeah, my world's falling apart for one thing." Sudi slumped into a chair and blinked back her tears. If she started crying, Meri and Dalila would rush to comfort her, and she didn't want more sympathy, because even the smallest gesture right now would open a floodgate that she would never be able to close again.

To distract herself from her rising emotions, she pulled her wand from the bag. The snake head knocked against her shoulder, sending a shock of pain down her back. After that, the wand tried to jerk itself away from her.

"The wand is testing you," Abdel said as she struggled to hold on to it. "You need to show it that you're in charge. Then it will respect you and follow your command."

"I doubt that," she said as she joined Meri and Dalila and waited for the lesson to begin.

"Challenge your enemy," Abdel said, starting the drill that they always used to warm up before they received new instructions.

Sudi grappled with her wand. It oscillated, almost hitting Abdel. He stepped back to a safer distance before he gave the next command: "Defend yourself from attack."

Tiny silver stars spurted from the end of Meri's wand and formed a protective shell around her. Dalila's shot out a fanfare of twinkling embers. The icy sparks swirled around her, enclosing her in a cocoon.

At the same time, a sickly orange glow had emanated from Sudi's wand. The light covered her and made her itch.

Abdel frowned at Sudi. "All right, let's try a very simple command. Set your wands down and call them back to you."

Sudi set her wand on the couch next to Dalila's and Meri's. Then she stood in line with her friends and lifted her hand, stretching her arm out, two fingers pointed.

With a speed that seemed impossible, two of the wands flew back. Dalila caught hers and twirled it happily. Meri tapped hers on the ground. Sudi's wand, however, remained obstinately where she had left it.

"Try again," Abdel encouraged.

Sudi stretched out her arm. This time the wand came rotating back to her.

"Yikes!" she yelled and ducked. The wand crashed into the wall behind her, causing a picture to fall.

"Well, at least it moved this time," Abdel said. "That's progress."

For more than an hour, Sudi tried without success to follow Abdel's commands. She had the impression that her wand despised her.

When the session finally ended, her arms ached, and blisters stung her palms.

"Meri and Dalila can leave," Abdel said, looking perturbed, "but, Sudi, I want you to stay until you can cast at least one spell correctly, and then you can go."

"It won't take you long," Meri said optimistically.

"We'll wait for you outside," Dalila added.

"Just go on," Sudi said, feeling hopeless. "I'll probably be here till midnight."

While Abdel said good-bye to Meri and Dalila at the door, the ghost breezed against Sudi, becoming semivisible. "Let me help you, mistress," she whispered.

"How?" Sudi asked in a low, hushed voice. "The wand is incorrigible. It won't do anything it doesn't want to do."

"We won't use the wand," the ghost giggled. "Just say what you want done and I'll do it."

Sudi smirked. "Okay."

As soon as Abdel came back, Sudi said, "I think I've got the hang of it now." She lifted her wand and said, "Move the chair."

In response, the chair skidded across the floor.

Abdel applauded and smiled proudly. "That's very difficult to do, especially without any instruction."

Sudi felt terrible for deceiving him, but her body was too sore to continue practicing.

"Very good," Abdel said, again showing his pleasure. "You're having a more difficult time with your wand because—"

"The magic within me is weaker," Sudi said sorrowfully.

"Not at all," Abdel countered. "It's because the magic inside you is so strong. You've been given a wand that is impossible for others to control. The power you have, when combined with that of your wand, is strong enough to move the stars."

"Me?" Sudi almost laughed.

"Don't you feel the energy inside you longing for expression?" he asked.

"I wish I did," she said bleakly, wondering if what Abdel had just told her could be true.

Abdel walked her to the door, and as she stepped outside, he added, "I know you don't believe me now, but some day, you'll know that I'm telling you the truth."

When he closed the door, she gazed up at the stars in wonder, then sighed, doubting what Abdel had told her. He had most likely wanted to encourage her so that she wouldn't feel as defeated as she did.

The ghost looped around her, interrupting her thoughts. "Let's do something to cheer you up," she murmured into Sudi's ear. "What makes you happy?"

Sudi thought about going dancing, but it was too early for any of the clubs to be open. Impulsively, she hailed a cab. She loved looking at the paintings in the National Gallery of Art, and a visit there always calmed her.

Minutes later, as she was handing the driver her last dollar bills, she realized that the museum was closing. People were streaming en masse down the front steps. She groaned, thinking about the long walk home, but then she saw Michelle crossing the Mall with Scott.

"What is it, mistress?" the ghost asked, seeming to sense her anger.

"Michelle," Sudi said.

"What do you want me to do to her?" The ghost sounded eager.

Horrible thoughts came to mind, surprising Sudi with their intensity. At last she said, "Nothing serious, just embarrass her."

The ghost twirled up, a whirlwind of giggles.

Moments later, Michelle's hair blew around her face. When she brushed it back, a dollop of mud fell on her head.

"*Eeww!*" she squealed and looked up into a

tree, then lost her balance and stumbled forward, landing in the grass. Mysteriously, more mud splattered on her face. When she opened her purse to take out a tissue, all the contents spilled out.

Scott knelt beside her and tried to help her pick up the lipstick and perfume, but she pushed him away.

"Don't look at me," she said, trying to hide her mud-caked face beneath her hair.

Completely flummoxed, Michelle grabbed her wallet and phone. Then, leaving her makeup and purse, she raced across the Mall to where her driver and car were waiting for her.

But the silly revenge didn't give Sudi the pleasure that she had imagined it would. She had always thought of Michelle as extremely self-centered, but now she saw the insecurity and fear behind her obnoxious behavior. Any other girl would have laughed if she had found herself caught in such a slapstick skit, but Michelle had no real confidence.

The ghost returned and traced her fingers through Sudi's hair. "Why aren't you pleased, mistress? Did I not do as you wished?"

"I made a mistake," Sudi said. "Go with

Michelle, and do something to make her happy again."

"I'll try, mistress." The ghost flew after Michelle, no more than a hint of vapor gliding through the air. Then, like a puff of smoke, she seeped into the car before the driver shut the door.

Sudi had been so focused on Michelle that she hadn't noticed Scott walking toward her until he was standing next to her.

"Sudi," Scott said, "I've wanted to talk to you ever since the other night. Can I walk you home?" He sounded like he was afraid she'd tell him no.

"It could take an hour," she said, giving him her best encouraging smile.

"I know," he answered. Then he noticed her bag. "Did you start playing sports?"

Sudi said the first thing that popped into her head: "Yeah, I'm really into street hockey."

He practically gasped. "You?"

She held out her hand to show him her blisters. "I have bruises, too," she said. "But it's too cold to show you here."

"Wow, that doesn't seem like you," he said.

"I'm full of surprises," she smirked.

After that, they fell into cautious conversation

that soon became natural and filled with laughter.

"So, how's the new boyfriend?" Scott asked as if the question had been on his mind for a long time. His huge grin didn't hide the hurt in his eyes.

"What was I supposed to think, Scott?" Sudi complained. "You never returned my calls."

He stopped. "Didn't Michelle tell you? My grandmother took away my cell phone, because I'd racked up such humongous charges calling my friends in California."

"She never told me," Sudi said. "But I suppose she did tell you that another guy was at my house."

"I couldn't believe that you had found someone else," he confessed. "I had to see for myself."

"And what was Michelle doing with you just now?" Sudi asked. "Telling you bad things about me, I imagine."

He nodded. "About Zack and Brian last night at the club." He stepped in front of her, his hands holding her arms. "I get it. I was stupid for trusting Michelle to give you the message. Sorry."

She smiled and nodded, happy to be with him again. But as they strolled down Massachusetts Avenue, she wondered how much she could trust her feelings in all this. When she was near Raul, he was the one she liked, but now that she was with Scott, his embrace was what she wanted. How could she be so impossibly fickle?

"I think someone's following us," Scott said, pulling her from her thoughts.

Sudi turned back. A large black dog padded across the street.

"I don't see anyone," she said.

But by the time they reached a construction site, an uneasy feeling was rising inside her. Her mother had always told her to trust her instincts, even if doing so resulted in irrational behavior. It was better to be embarrassed than to end up dead.

"Let's hide until we can see who it is," Sudi said.

"Hide?" Scott looked unsure but he didn't argue.

The wire mesh fence jangled noisily as they squeezed through an opening. They snuck into the construction site, then stepped quickly behind a stack of gray bricks.

"You're trembling." Scott put his arms around Sudi, and when his lips touched hers, a pleasant ache rushed through her but even the sweet longing for more kisses wasn't enough to distract her from the strange sense of foreboding that had taken hold of her.

She opened her eyes and caught something moving in the shadows behind Scott. At the same moment, the wind whipped the plastic covering off the bricks and snapped it around them. Maybe that was all the movement had been, a sudden gust of wind racing through the dark and moving coverings.

"Let's go inside," Scott whispered against her cheek, his breath warm and enticing. When she didn't move, he added, "Someplace warm."

She glanced back at the building, alert, unable to quell her apprehension. She had been foolish. They should have stayed on the street. "Maybe we should leave."

"I thought you wanted to kiss me." His fingers had found their way inside her coat and were on her waist, teasing and pulling her back to him.

"I do, but . . ." She looked into his eyes, wondering how she could tell him, without sounding wacky, that she was worried about saving their lives.

"I don't want you to get into more trouble with your grandmother," Sudi said. "Let's go."

He pulled her back toward him. "I don't even know why I try to understand you. It's like you're testing me, trying to see how weird you can act before I tell you we're through."

She knew what was coming next. "Don't say it."

"I don't need to. You've already found another boyfriend, so I guess you broke up with me." He headed back the way they had come. A blast of wind suddenly lifted his coat, waving it into a tangle behind him.

"Scott, just wait for me. I can explain," Sudi said, though her mind was blank and she was unable to come up with a lie.

Without looking back, Scott pushed through the opening in the fence.

She picked up her bag and started to run after him, then froze as the distinct scent that she had smelled on Zack the night before filled the air.

Zack stepped over the slurry, a hardened mound of leftover concrete, and walked toward her. "I wouldn't worry about Scott. You've got bigger problems right now."

CHAPTER 10

Loud tapping startled Sudi and she turned away from Zack. Behind her, she saw Garrett jump onto a pallet of wood and beat out a fast stomping rhythm. "Hey, Sudi," he said grimly, an odd, sly look in his eyes.

Nick swung down from the scaffolding above her. The tail of his black coat fanned over her. "You're not at school now," he warned.

Anticipating an attack, she fell to her knees, opened the sports bag, and took out her wand. She faced her enemies, scowling in concentration. But they didn't look afraid, or even worried. Her poor wand skills were probably a running joke among cult members.

Nick shot an impatient glance back at Zack. "Can't we just go for her?"

Sudi drew a jagged breath, her heart racing.

"Wait," Zack answered. "I want to see what she can do."

Sudi dramatically raised her wand above her head, waving it around even though her arms were trembling, and praying to get the words right this time. "*Sen na her ari neken a!*" she shouted. A spray of white stars swept around her, surprising her as much as it did the three of them.

Garrett stepped back.

"Dang!" Nick became wide-eyed, ready to run.

Even Zack looked startled. He stood up straight, his back rigid.

Her words had made them wary. Confident now, with silvery embers whirling around her, Sudi added, "*Maa-F baka a.*"

The wand jiggled back and forth, then struck Sudi in the head.

"Ouch!" she yelled as pain raced through her.

Nick grinned. Garrett did a double take, then laughed alongside his friends.

"You asked the wand to make you strong against us," Zack explained. "And then you told it to show us your feebleness." He studied her as she rubbed the bump that was swelling on her head. "Why did they ever choose you?" he asked.

Sudi didn't take offense. Their hysterics were giving her the opportunity she needed. Pretending to be on the verge of tears, she sniffled, then watched them carefully. While they were busy making fun of her clumsy magic, she spun around and raced toward the building, her wand swinging wildly in her hand.

When she darted behind a sign that read, CAUTION: HARD HATS REQUIRED, their laughter stopped.

"Get her," Zack yelled.

Her feet skidded on the grit covering the floor as she stopped to get her bearings. Stacks of insulation hid her for the moment. She tried the door to what looked like an office, hoping to find a phone inside. The door was locked; what was worse, jiggling the latch had given away her location.

"She's over there!" Garrett called out.

Sudi raced down a hallway, her boots hitting the bare concrete hard. A line of incandescent lights in orange plastic cages hung from the crossbeams overhead. She needed to find darkness in which to hide. Going as fast as she dared, she followed a thick black cable up a stairwell to the next floor.

The cable was a gas line that fueled a large tube. Slanted at an angle, it looked like the muzzle on a cannon that was pointed at her. A fire burned inside at the bottom. The roar of the flames was intense, and so was the heat as she carefully slipped around the heater.

"Sudi!" Nick shouted.

She glanced back as Nick pointed her out to the others. All three charged toward her.

Their footsteps thundered after her as she dashed up the next flight of stairs, then, abruptly, the noise stopped when she reached the landing. The silence was worse. What were they planning?

Going sideways now so that she could see both ends of the hallway, she stole past an empty elevator shaft. Their urgent whispers came up to her from the floor below. She listened, trying to make out their plan.

". . . Get her," Garrett hissed. "It'll be easier if we do it Zack's way."

"Then we'll make her one of us," Nick snickered in a low voice.

Sudi shuddered. She didn't understand what they were talking about, but she had the distinct impression that it was something far worse than becoming a cult member.

She needed to hide. She hurried into a room where plastic covered the unfinished walls. The clear giant sheets rippled and swelled and let in the icy wind.

Shivering, Sudi paused. An odd sense of something moving behind her made her turn. Just for a moment, she thought she had seen a four-legged beast. Maybe a guard dog was sniffing around, trying to locate the intruders. Not wanting to be the one caught, she maneuvered through the metal framing into the next room. Then, holding her wand against her, she eased into a small gap between stacks of drywall and squatted down, terrified that the others could hear her labored breathing. She bit on her sleeve to quiet her chattering teeth and kept her head down, hoping that that would be enough to conceal the vapor made by her breath.

Moments later, when the sharp scent of Zack's cologne filled the air, she crouched down even lower. A scuffing sound made her glance up as Zack stepped past her. She pressed her wand tight against her, afraid it would choose that moment to jump. This time, it remained still.

After Zack left the room, she slowly let out her breath. Her nose and eyes were watering from the cold, and already the stinging pain in her face and hands was agonizing. She needed to find her way back to one of the heaters, and then, maybe, if she was lucky, she could sneak back out of the building while Zack and his friends were searching for her on the higher floors.

She crept carefully out and stole around piles of scaffolding, then hurried to a gas heater at the end of the hallway. The jetting flames rumbled at the bottom of the tube. She held her hands out, knowing she was vulnerable, and stared at the circle of blue fire.

Warm at last, she continued on, but when she reached the stairwell, she caught a glimpse of Nick coming up the steps from the floor below. Nerves thrumming, she rushed across the landing before he could see her. Then, keeping her back pressed against the wall, she stealthily made her way to the next floor, where the only lights came from the street below. She didn't know what would happen to her wand, but she could no longer worry about taking care of it. She hoped Abdel would understand, because the only option left to her was to change into a bird to escape.

The plastic sheeting at the doorway behind her moved out, then in, as if someone had passed by it on the other side. She turned slowly, confused at first by what she saw. Within the dim shadows, the darker image of a dog slinked past the opening, but it advanced with the graceful movement of a feline. Mesmerized, she stared at the strange animal and didn't hear Zack until he was only a few feet away from her.

CHAPTER 11

"Guess we caught you now." Garrett stepped from the darkness joining Zack. Nick followed after him with slow, lazy steps.

A smile crept over Sudi's face. Maybe it was the cold, or exhaustion, or the hunger she saw in their eyes. But she was resolute. No way were they taking her without a fight.

As if reading her thoughts, Nick lunged forward and tried to grab her.

Sudi jumped back. "Do you think I'm going to

go down all girlie and sweet?" she yelled as rage filled her chest. "I'm taking some DNA with me, so the police can identify my attackers."

She gripped her wand with both hands and swung it like a baseball bat.

Winded from the chase, Nick wasn't as quick as the other two. The tip of the snake head got him.

He yelled and grabbed his mouth.

"I barely *nicked* you, Nick," Sudi taunted. Her fingers twitched, anxious for another swing. She loved the adrenaline rush. "Batter up!" She yelled, eyeing them, daring them to step forward.

Garrett inched toward her. When she lunged at him, swinging, Zack leapt forward and caught her wand in the palm of his hand.

She expected him to cry out in pain. Instead, he stared at her, his eyes serious, his lips forming a thin smile.

For a moment, the warrior inside her had risen, but now it was gone. She bit her lip to keep from whimpering.

"Mistress!" a worried voice filled the air.

Sudi looked up. Her ghost had returned and

was rushing down to attack. A long, shrill cry came out of her mouth.

Nick screamed and fell back against Garrett, his face contorted in terror. Garrett pushed him away, then spun around and ran. Clumsily, Nick turned and ran after him.

The ghost charged at Zack, but he remained more intrigued than afraid, even when she brushed a hand through him, and that worried Sudi.

"I've seen a ghost before," he said to the apparition. "You don't scare me."

"What should we do, mistress?" The ghost drifted back and clung to Sudi. "Do you have a plan?"

Sudi nodded, even though she didn't have a clue. But while she was thinking, she needed to do something to distract Zack. "Why did you become a cult member?" she asked, stalling.

"I love the power," he replied, stepping toward her. "I can harm the people who have tormented me." His hands reached out and touched her hair.

In response she eased away from him and immediately realized that she had been standing too close to the edge. The security wire stopped her fall, but her feet were teetering on the brink.

She inched forward. "So you joined the cult to get revenge?"

"I didn't join," he confessed. "The cult leaders took my soul."

"They forced you?" Sudi asked, surprised. "What did they do to you?"

"If you're so interested, join the cult and find out." Zack leaned closer, and for a moment she thought he was going to kiss her. Instinctively, she drew back. The wire wobbled against her back. This time she lost her footing. The safety wire scraped the back of her head, and she fell.

The ghost tried to catch Sudi, but she plunged on through her, barreling down.

"Amun-Re, eldest of the gods," she muttered breathlessly, her heart hammering.

With total concentration, she thought the remaining words: *Mysterious power of wind, make a path for me to change my earthly* khat *into that of beloved Bennu.* Xu kua. *I am glorious.* User Kua. *I am mighty.* Neteri kua. *I am strong.*

Her wings shot out, ripping through her sweater and coat, and frantically slapped the air, but there was enough time only to slow her descent. When her feet hit the ground, the pain was immense. She lost her balance and staggered forward. The wand landed beside her, clattering noisily.

Feathers, yarn, and bits of her tattered leather coat rained down on top of her. She folded her wings behind her and glanced up.

Zack stood on the edge, gripping the safety wire and watching her. "You're amazing, Sudi!" he yelled. His words echoed out into the night.

"Mistress, we need to leave quickly," the ghost insisted, taking Sudi's attention away from Zack. "I hear others coming."

Woozy and nauseated, Sudi picked up the wand. She grimaced from the pain, then stopped, unable to step forward. Dizziness overcame her and just as she became aware of other voices and approaching footsteps, she passed out.

CHAPTER 12

Sudi awakened to find herself in her own bed, wearing Meri's sweater and swaddled in blankets, a bitter taste in her mouth. Dalila was seated on a chair close by, holding a glass of water. Meri sat cross-legged on the bed, dressed in frayed jeans and a lacy camisole.

Blearily, Sudi glanced up.

A hazy form ruffled the valance above the window. Then the ghost's face materialized within the nebulous shape and smiled down at her before vanishing.

"Drink this." Dalila handed Sudi the glass of water. "The spell I had to put on you can leave a sour taste in your mouth."

Sudi gulped down the cold water. "How did you find me?" she asked when she had finished.

Dalila took the glass back and set it on the nightstand. "We wanted to share the macaroons and tea with you, but when we went back to Abdel's house, he told us that you had left already."

"So we started looking for you," Meri added with an impish grin. "Luckily, we ran into Scott on his way home."

"I can just imagine what he said about me." Sudi groaned as she shifted her weight. The intensity of the pain in her arms and back surprised her.

"Scott told us he'd left you at a construction site," Dalila said.

"He was upset because you were acting strange, wanting to kiss him, then suddenly changing your mind and not," Meri giggled. "But we knew you were in trouble. It didn't take much to figure out that you were trying to save his life, not make out with him."

The door to the bedroom opened and Mrs.

Finders poked her head inside. "I just got off the phone with your mother," she said. "I told her that it's a miracle you didn't break any bones." Mrs. Finders paused. "I've never heard of a girl playing street hockey before, but your mother was delighted to hear that you are."

"How did you lose your coat *and* your sweater?" Nicole asked, peering in from behind the housekeeper.

"Her clothes became wet," Dalila lied smoothly. "I made her take them off so she wouldn't catch a cold."

"I let her borrow my sweater," Meri said, continuing the false story. "Then I forgot to take her clothes with us when we left. It's my fault, really, that her coat and sweater are lost. I'm sure my mother will buy her new ones."

Carrie remained solemn, obviously not believing their lies. "Where are your skates and hockey stick?"

"I forgot those, too," Meri said with a beaming smile.

Mrs. Finders shook her head. "You're playing the game too hard. If you were my daughter, I wouldn't let you play at all."

When the door closed again, Sudi stared at Dalila, then Meri. "Street hockey?" she asked.

In response, Meri playfully poked her and said, "It was your lie first."

"Scott told us that you had blisters and bruises from playing street hockey," Dalila laughed. "We guessed that you'd told him that to cover for what your wand had done to your hands and arms."

"So we used the same lie to explain to Mrs. Finders why we were helping you home," Meri said. "You looked pretty bad."

Dalila pulled three Styrofoam cups from a paper bag and set them in a line on the nightstand. "Meri's driver brought us here, but I had to put a spell on you to make you conscious enough to walk up the stairs."

"You were still acting all loopy and silly," Meri said.

"You passed out again once we got you into your room," Dalila added, removing the plastic lids from the cups. A spicy aroma wafted into the air.

"We didn't think a hospital would be a very safe place for you until we found out what had happened." Meri suddenly looked somber. "We didn't make a mistake, did we? You are all right, aren't you?"

Sudi nodded. "Just sore." Then she smiled. "Street hockey. I can't wait for that one to get around school."

Dalila handed her the tea. "But what did happen at the construction site?"

"You said you had fallen off the building," Meri explained.

Sudi gratefully sipped the sweet brew. "I thought Zack was going to kiss me, so I stepped back and fell."

"Zack?" Meri and Dalila said in unison.

Sudi thought for a moment. "I guess there's a lot I need to tell you."

"Tell us now." Dalila opened a box and offered her a macaroon.

Sudi took a cookie and slowly began telling Meri and Dalila about the way Zack and his friends had been tormenting her at school. She carefully left out any mention of the ghost, feeling it was better to keep that secret for a while.

When she had finished, Meri said, "I thought

that kids were lured into joining the cult by false promises, but if Zack was taken against his will, then there must be a way that we can release him, and others like him."

"My thoughts exactly," Sudi agreed. "I think we should go to The Jackal and do some investigating."

"I'll bet if we snooped around in some of those back rooms we could find out what's being done to make kids become cult members," Meri said.

"But we need to talk to Abdel first," Dalila cautioned.

"Why?" Sudi asked.

"Because we have a more urgent threat," Dalila explained. "We have to find out what is affecting the cosmos and making the stars change position."

"You're right." Sudi nodded and swallowed the last drop of her tea, cold now, but still soothing.

Dalila looked suddenly anxious. "Don't do anything impulsive," she warned.

"Like what?" Sudi asked defensively.

"Like, don't go to The Jackal on your own to investigate," Meri said. "Promise."

"I promise," Sudi said earnestly, but already a plan was forming in her mind.

Friday night, Sudi hurried down F Street in the Penn Quarter, the tapping of her high-heeled boots echoing off the sidewalk. When she heard the music from inside The Jackal, she slipped off her dad's old fishing jacket and let it fall to the ground. Leaving it there, she strutted down the street as if she owned the night.

Three guys drinking beers called out to her and made lewd remarks from the cab of a parked truck.

Outraged, the ghost accompanying Sudi zoomed through the open window and, in a fit of anger, spilled their drinks on their laps, then zipped back, still invisible, and joined Sudi again.

"How'd she do that?" the guy with the goatee asked.

"She didn't," the one with the sleeve tattoos argued back. "You did it, because you were gawking at her and not watching what you were doing."

Sudi smiled smugly and continued past them. At one time their stares would have intimidated her, but now she knew the real danger for a girl alone at night in D.C. and she was on her way to face it.

As she got closer to The Jackal, music from inside the club vibrated outside, competing with the pounding bass from cars that rolled slowly by checking out the crowd. She fidgeted with her sequined cami and pulled out the All Access pass from the pocket of her jeans. The club owner, who was also the leader of the cult, had given her the pass, not as a perk, but as a way to taunt her and show her how little he feared her. She felt certain that he had never expected her actually to use it, but it was definitely going to help her now.

She strode past the long line of kids waiting to go inside, then cut into the front and flashed her pass. The security guard with the headset waved her through.

As she moved around the gilded wood figures of pharaohs, she murmured a spell, *"An arit sen tet er a."* Then, remembering the mistake she had made with her wand, she quickly said the words in English: "May they not do evil to me."

Immediately, the air glimmered in front of her. She stepped through the wavering light and strolled down the golden-brick passageway of the entrance corridor. Beyond the statues of reclining black jackals, two bare-chested men dressed like ancient Egyptians waited for her. When she reached them, they opened a second set of doors that whooshed shut behind her.

Overhead, the vaulted ceiling gave the illusion of a starry night sky. She waited until her eyes adjusted to the dim light.

The ghost pressed against her. "You're safe with me, mistress."

Sudi had a strange feeling that the ghost was

uneasy. "What do you sense here?"

"Evil," the ghost breathed. "Terrible evil, mistress."

A continuous rhythmic humming filled the air. A new band had taken the stage and was exciting the crowd with the rising thunder of the drums. Sudi hurried down a ramp that led out into a vast dance floor. Laser lights ripped through the air as the hard-hitting music began. Kids screamed and clapped and started dancing.

Sudi slid into the crowd, scanning the faces, and threaded her way through the dancers. When she reached the other side of the room, a door marked PRIVATE, MEMBERS ONLY opened. Light from inside spilled out across the couples leaning against the wall kissing.

Tension rippled through Sudi's back. The club owner stood in the doorway. Dressed in an expensive, tailored suit, he wore a gold ankh around his neck. The T-shaped cross with the looping handle was the symbol of life and divine immortality, and it kept him alive. Sudi had torn the talisman off him once and watched him turn to dust. She never wanted to witness that again.

Zack, Garrett, and Nick joined the club

owner. A girl was with them, dressed in a red satin tunic and skinny black jeans. Sudi didn't recognize her at first. Then the girl looked up at Zack and the light caught her face.

Sudi's stomach took a dive. Sara was with Zack.

The club owner stood back and invited them into the room. Sudi watched, her heart racing, and then she remembered her ghost.

"Stay with Sara and make sure nothing happens to her," Sudi said.

In response, the ghost whispered into Sudi's ear, "Mistress, I promise not to let them harm her."

A few seconds later, Sara's hair swept up in a gentle wave before settling on her shoulders again. By that motion, Sudi knew the ghost was with her.

Unexpectedly, Zack turned and glanced back, as if he had sensed her watching him. Sudi ducked behind three girls dancing together.

As soon as the door closed, she took a deep breath and ran toward it, determined to rescue Sara. When her fingers circled the doorknob, someone touched her shoulder. She winced and drew back, her heart pounding even heavier.

Raul put his arm around her and pulled her

toward the dance floor. "I called your house, but your mom said you couldn't go out yet." He ran his finger over her bruises. "She said you'd hurt yourself playing street hockey."

"That's why I wasn't at school." Her anxiety was rising. She needed to make sure Sara was all right.

"Let's dance," Raul said, but his eyes looked eager to do more than dance.

She gave him a flirty smile. "Go get us something to drink, and meet me back over there."

He looked in the direction she was pointing. "The other side of the dance floor?"

She pressed against him. "It's darker over there. Get the drinks and come find me."

"Come with me," he said. "I don't want to leave you."

She kissed his cheek and hoped he didn't sense the way she was trembling. "I promise I won't dance with anyone else while you're gone." She gave him a sultry look. "Hurry."

A wicked smile stretched over his face. "I'll be right back."

As soon as Raul left, she charged back to the

door. Without hesitating, she opened it, stepped inside, and hurriedly glanced around.

The room was dark, lit only by the lights from video screens. A buffet table loaded with food was pressed against one wall. Heavy velvet curtains covered what was apparently another doorway, but nothing seemed unusual except for the overpowering scent of Zack's cologne. The large space didn't even look like part of the club, but more like someone's basement recreation room.

After a moment, Sudi realized that she could no longer hear the band; only a slight tremor from the pounding beat. That unnerved her. What reason would the cult have for a soundproof room, except to keep the partygoers on the other side of the wall from hearing someone's screams for help?

More cautious now, she eased over to the buffet table and surveyed the room. Apparently, no one had seen her enter; or if they had, they hadn't been able to recognize her in the dim light. Maybe they had assumed she was a cult member. She picked up a brownie and pretended to be absorbed in eating it.

Sara stood on a mat that was placed on the

floor in front of a screen. Four arrows surrounded each of her feet, pointing up, down, left, and right.

Garrett tapped the mat. In response, song titles began scrolling down the screen. "Try this one," he said. "It's a good one for beginners."

The music started.

Sara attempted to follow the arrows that rolled up and over the stationary ones at the top of the screen, but her feet didn't hit the matching arrows on the mat. She laughed at her mistakes and stumbled forward.

Zack caught her and kissed her temple.

"Try again," Garrett said. "Don't concentrate on the arrows at the top. The best way to do the footing is to watch the arrows that are coming up, see which way they're pointing."

"But on the machine, it says to step once the arrows hit the top," Sara complained.

"I know, but don't." Garrett smiled. "If you concentrate on the top arrows, you're going to mess up."

"It's confusing." Sara leaned back against Zack. He whispered something into her ear.

"Let me show you." Garrett stepped onto the

mat. The arrows began scrolling, and when they rolled over the stationary ones at the top, his feet hit the matching ones on the mat.

Sudi watched, fascinated by Garrett's precision, then other movement made her glance away. Zack and Sara were pushing through the drapery leaving the room.

Not knowing what she would find, Sudi crept after them, pulled the soft velvet aside, and peeked down a water-stained corridor. The door at the other end was already closing.

Her uneasiness suddenly sharpened into fear, not for herself, but for Sara. She sprinted down the hallway, arms pumping at her sides.

"Sara!" she screamed, no longer caring who discovered her in the restricted area of the club.

She flung open the door and stepped outside into a narrow alley.

A car sped away from her, the taillights casting a red glow over the exhaust. Then, with a screech of tires, the car turned onto the street and disappeared.

"Sara," Sudi said, feeling her shoulders slump.

The door opened behind her. Immediately a

strange energy gathered around her, oddly warm in the cold night air. Her body tensed. She turned and stared up into the baleful eyes of the club owner.

"Did you come here looking for someone, Sudi?" he asked unpleasantly. "Your friend Sara, perhaps?"

Sudi glared at him.

"She's quite attracted to Zack. In fact, he persuaded her to become a member of the cult tonight. She'll enjoy the spa, don't you think?" He laughed at her, turned, and walked back inside, slamming the door.

A heavy despair settled over Sudi. How was she going to rescue Sara now?

CHAPTER 14

At home in bed later, Sudi leaned against her pillows absentmindedly fiddling with her cell phone. An hour earlier, she had given up any hope that the ghost would return and help her. In desperation, she had even tried to use her wand to locate Sara, but the bronze rod had remained unaffected by her pleas, the hieroglyphs immobile.

She sighed heavily and put the phone down. Dalila was still out of range. She had gone with her uncle and Abdel away from the city lights to gaze up at the stars. And Meri was in New York City at some fund-raiser with her mother, her cell phone turned off. That left Sudi alone. She didn't know what to do.

The roar of a car engine roused her from her thoughts. She jumped off her bed and looked out the window. Brian's Cadillac rolled down the alley and parked where he had always waited for her when she used to sneak out to meet him.

Heartened, and confident that the goddess Isis was using him again, Sudi threw on her old jeans and sweatshirt, then tugged on her socks and tennis shoes.

She opened her bedroom door and listened. When she heard her father's snoring, she crept from her room and moved quietly down the hallway, descended the stairs, then left the house through the back porch, shutting but not locking the door.

Brian gunned the engine in welcome when he saw her racing toward him. She jumped into the car.

"Where are we going?" she asked, buckling herself in.

"Virginia," he answered as he slammed his foot on the accelerator.

The car shot forward, throwing Sudi back in her seat.

For a moment she wondered if she had made a mistake. Maybe Brian wanted an adrenaline high. She glanced behind her. His skates weren't there, but that didn't mean they weren't in the trunk. Brian was into skitching and car surfing—anything extreme. How many times had he forced her to speed down the back roads in Virginia while he wore his skates and held on to the bumper?

She leaned forward and gazed up at his face. His eyes were wide, unblinking; he was definitely spellbound.

They rode in silence across the bridge spanning the Potomac and continued on until the houses became sparse and the only light came from the car and the moon. Then, without warning, Brian turned off the highway. The car's headlights swept over a line of trees covered with dead vines.

Sudi braced herself for a crash. But Brian grappled with the steering wheel, turning it until the wheels found an old country road. Branches scraped over the hood and slapped against the windshield as they blasted forward.

They had traveled another mile when, abruptly, Brian stopped the car.

The indicator lights on the dashboard lit his face, and when he turned to look at her, Sudi had the strong sensation that Isis was the one gazing at her. "This is where you need to be," Brian said.

"Here?" she asked.

Isolated and remote, the woodland looked impenetrable. Dead vines twisted around the tree trunks, and prickly shrubs covered the forest floor. Overhead, the interlaced branches caught the moonlight and cast enough shadow to make the darkness forbidding.

"I thought you wanted to rescue Sara," Brian scolded before he killed the engine.

Without waiting for her, he opened the car door, got out, and started walking, crunching twigs and leaves beneath his feet.

Sudi jumped out of the car and plodded after him. "Wait up."

A bramble snagged her sweatshirt. When she stopped to unhook herself from the scrambling bush, Brian turned back and frowned.

"We're running out of time." He shook his head in disgust and galumphed into the forest.

She rushed after him. The air was cold and filled with unfamiliar scents. She pulled the sleeves of her sweatshirt over her hands and hiked forward.

Clouds scudded across the sky as a harsh wind howled through the trees. Branches creaked, and dead leaves skittered around her. Through those sounds, came a thrumming, definitely a man-made noise that grew louder as she and Brian went deeper into the woods.

"What is that buzzing?" she asked. "Do you think campers are running a generator to keep themselves warm?"

"Be quiet," Brian whispered.

After a short distance, he pointed ahead to where the trees were silhouetted against a flickering glow.

Slowly, Sudi eased forward, her heart hammering. She pressed her cheek against the rough bark of a tree and then cautiously peered around it.

Statues of the god Seth flanked a gateway

between two pillars. The deities had a man's body but the head of a strange animal with rectangular ears and a long snout. The artist in ancient times was probably portraying a mythical beast whose identity had later been lost in time, but the only creature in existence today that remotely resembled the animal was the anteater.

Something dark moved near the base of the statue, and when Sudi leaned forward to see what it was, Brian clasped his hand over her mouth and caught her scream.

Animals, but not like any she had ever seen before, prowled gracefully in a clearing. Their shoulder bones jutted oddly, pushing the skin out at sharp angles on their backs. Their pointed muzzles intensified their evil appearance. The creatures reminded her of the sleek black statues of the jackals that lined the entrance to The Jackal, only these were terrifyingly beautiful and fiercely alive.

The ears of the one closest to her twitched. The animal stopped moving, and its head turned toward her hiding place.

She dug her face into Brian's shoulder and held her breath, certain the animal could hear her heartbeat and smell her fear. She tensed, waiting for teeth to rip through her neck.

When nothing happened, she opened her eyes again.

Brian released her and took her hand. With trepidation, she followed him across an undulating pattern of stones that made a path through the forest. Then they hid again, near a headless black animal skin hung from a pole.

Chanting began, and then one voice rose above the others.

"The bloodstained are welcome here," the voice said. "Seth, who brought murder into the world, is the protector of the damned."

Hidden behind the trees, Sudi crawled forward and crouched behind a shrub.

The club owner, now dressed as a priest, in a cloak made from leopard skins, stood in an inner court lit with the flames burning in oil lamps set on pedestals. On his chest he wore a pectoral ornament depicting Seth, along with the gold ankh. His shaved head seemed to shimmer in the moonlight. With a jolt, Sudi realized the circle of light was emanating from inside him.

A flash of red caught her attention. She inched forward to see the congregation better. Men and women—old and young, all dressed in white—stood in the clearing, warmed by portable heaters running on generators—which explained the flashing red light. They parted and made way for Zack and Sara, who were walking up to the priest.

Sara looked dazed, her glossy hair now tangled and unkempt. Sudi saw no evidence that the ghost was still with her.

The priest lifted a canopic jar.

Dalila had told Sudi that the containers were used to hold the internal organs that were removed from the body before it was mummified, but Sudi had a sinking feeling that the priest intended to take something far more precious from Sara.

A twig snapped behind her. Sudi ignored the noise. She had to do something to save Sara, but her mind was numb with panic and couldn't come up with a plan.

The priest placed his hand on Sara's head. A strange aura emanated from his fingers.

Then he spoke: "*Du ut des.*"

Sudi had heard the priest say those words

before. Sara was going to be given in sacrifice.

"What the—?" Brian yelled suddenly.

Sudi looked behind her, her heartbeat thundering in her ears. She had been concentrating on Sara and hadn't noticed that Isis had lost control of Brian.

The priest released his hold on Sara, and, in the same moment, the chanting stopped. Ominous silence followed.

"Where the hell am I?" Brian blustered. Baffled and angry, he stared at the congregants, frowning as if he thought *they* had brought him out to the woods.

One of the doglike creatures crept toward him. Growling deep in its throat, it bared its horrible teeth.

Instinct kicked in, and Brian spun around and raced into the forest.

Members of the congregation shouted to each other. They couldn't let their secret be exposed. As one, they charged after Brian. Even Zack sprinted forward, leaving Sara alone with the priest.

That gave Sudi the opportunity she needed. Even though fear was rising inside her, she sprang from her hiding place beneath the shrub and tore into the clearing, knocking over a lamp. Flames spread across the oil spilling over the bricks.

The priest looked up, surprised to see Sudi, but then he smirked, "I'm glad you decided to join us."

Sudi grabbed Sara's hand. Her palm was cold and wet, the fingers lifeless.

"Come on," Sudi pleaded, her anxiety rising. "Follow me."

Sara remained motionless and continued staring blankly ahead.

"You see," the priest said smoothly, "Sara doesn't want to leave."

In desperation, Sudi yanked Sara forward. She stumbled and fell hard on the bricks, then lay sprawled out, licking the blood on her lip.

"Sudi!" she yelled, fear and relief colliding in her expression. The fall had broken whatever spell had been placed over her. She pulled herself up.

"You won't get away." The priest smiled cruelly and shouted a command.

Sara dug her fingers into Sudi's hand. "He's calling the animals. I saw them hunt down a man." Her jagged breathing broke her words apart.

Sudi pulled Sara forward, and they darted into the trees. Eerie howling from the animals echoed through the forest as the girls crashed through the underbrush and brackish water. Cold mud spattered over them.

"Brian's car is parked straight ahead," Sudi gasped. Then, letting go of Sara, she added, "Wait for him. When he gets there, both of you, leave."

"Without you? No way." Sara lunged forward and tried to grab Sudi's hand. "Those animals will—"

"It's stupid for both of us to die!" Sudi yelled, already starting to run back the way they had come, toward the howling animals.

Sudi didn't see the branch until it snapped across her face. Her eyes watered and she stumbled into an evergreen. Exhausted, a bruise swelling on her cheek, she regained her balance, but as she turned, fierce snarling surrounded her. The creatures had found her.

CHAPTER 15

The animals, as a group, came slinking toward Sudi, their rapacious desire to kill her blazing in their unbearably cruel eyes.

The largest creature advanced, its muscles supple with a predator's grace. When its paw swiped her arm, Sudi flinched but didn't feel any pain, only the warmth of blood trickling down her skin. The sleeve of her sweatshirt hung in tattered shreds.

A shrill cry made the creatures look up and

whimper. Nostrils flaring, they pointed their snouts into the air and tried to identify the scent of whatever was coming. Then, hunkered together, they cowered, whining, and pulled back.

At first, Sudi didn't see anything overhead. Then, a burst of wind slammed into her, knocking her back. Her hair whipped into her eyes as shadows swept around her with dizzying speed.

Keening, the creatures drew closer together and backed away from Sudi.

Another sudden gust lifted moldering leaves and spun them into a column, filling the night with the scent of decay and putrid, wet soil. Within the storm, the ghost appeared and, as the wind settled, stretched protectively in front of Sudi, shrieking at the mewling animals.

As one the predators turned and rushed away, their wails echoing through the forest. For the briefest moment, Sudi thought some of the creatures had transformed into people.

The ghost turned, undulating in front of Sudi. "I won't let the animals have you."

"Thank you," Sudi whispered with sudden relief.

"Thank me?" The ghost's delicate translucent face no longer appeared gentle and kind, but angry. "I won't let them have you because I will destroy you. I am your most determined enemy now."

"You?" Sudi pressed back against a tree.

"The cult leader has shown me that you alone are the cause of the wandering stars." The ghost's voice trembled with rage. "While I was serving you, you were betraying me and the world. The priest explained everything to me."

"You can't trust him," Sudi argued. "He's devoted his existence to evil."

"Should I trust you, mistress?" the ghost asked sharply. "You are the one with the power to move the stars."

"You've seen me try to work magic with my wand," Sudi said. "I don't know how. I can't!"

The ghost floated toward Sudi. "Your skills in deceit are masterful, but your deception no longer works on me. I know who you truly are, and you won't succeed."

"At what?" Sudi demanded.

The ghost didn't answer but calmly went on, "I'll have your body soon, and no one will ever know that you are no longer in control of it."

"My body?" Sudi breathed. "You mean, possess me?"

"Say good-bye to your life." After that, the ghost flew away, a wisp of moonlit vapor gliding through the trees.

Sudi stood in silence for a moment. Then, unexpectedly, footsteps crashed through the forest. Members of the congregation had probably located her. Or, maybe, the animals had watched the ghost leave and were racing back to finish their slaughter.

Shivering from cold and fear, she lumbered forward. When her legs became too wobbly to continue, she hid against a tree. Through the pine needles, she stared up at the stars and prayed for help. She didn't want to die or, worse, have her soul taken from her.

CHAPTER 16

Sara and Brian tromped through the underbrush, breathing loudly. They hadn't left Sudi after all. Relief rushed through her.

"I'm here!" Sudi cried out, trying to draw their attention to her, but her voice was weak, her throat dry, and her cry for help came out as a low, weak sound. Unsteadily, she stepped from her hiding place.

Sara saw her first and rushed to her. "We've been looking for you." She hugged Sudi, holding her tight. "You can't imagine what I was afraid had happened."

"Let's get out of here before those creatures come back," Brian said.

Sudi nodded and tried to walk. When she faltered, Brian caught her and scooped her into his arms. She had always known that he was an athlete, but his strength amazed her now. Big and clumsy in the classroom, he ran with grace and skill through the forest.

When they stepped out onto the dirt road where the Cadillac was parked, Brian set Sudi down and opened the car door. Sara scrambled inside, and Sudi slid in next to her.

"This is why you've been acting so weird lately, isn't it?" Sara said shakily as Brian got into the car. "You've known what the cult really is, and that's the reason you told me to stay away from Zack."

Sudi nodded.

"You should have told me everything." Sara sniffled.

"Would you have believed me?" Sudi asked.

"No," Sara answered, wiping her tears with

the hem of her top. "I don't even believe it now. It's too surreal."

"A frigging nightmare," Brian added.

A metallic clicking made Sudi lean forward to see what was causing the sound. Brian was trembling so badly that he couldn't fit the key into the ignition. Sudi grasped his hand to steady him, his fingers as cold as her own. The key slid in, and moments later, the engine turned over. Brian hit the accelerator and maneuvered a huge U-turn. The wheels bumped over the ruts, tossing Sudi back and forth against her seat. After that, the car sped forward. Thin tree branches ticked over the hood and windshield.

Brian increased their speed as they neared the highway. His eyes kept flicking to the rearview mirror.

Sudi gazed out the back window. She had expected the cult members to chase them, but so far no headlights were visible behind them.

"You have to tell us," Sara said unevenly. She had begun hiccuping between her sobs.

Sudi nervously brushed her fingers through her hair. Bits of dead leaves fell onto her lap. She stared down at them, trying to decide. She had to tell Brian and Sara something, and a lie wouldn't cut it this time.

"Isis and Seth have been in a struggle since ancient times," Sudi began.

"Jeez, is this going to be a history lesson?" Brian asked and glanced at her.

"It's a story about good versus evil," Sara said, nudging Brian. "I know a lot about Egyptian mythology. Osiris married the goddess Isis."

Sudi nodded. "Together they ruled Egypt until Seth became jealous and killed Osiris. Then Seth took over the throne."

"What does that have to do with what happened tonight?" Brian asked impatiently. "I mean those psychos back there were dressed like they thought they were living in ancient Egypt, but—"

"Let her talk," Sara interrupted, her voice still trembling.

"It's related," Sudi said. "Isis stole the Book of Thoth from the gods and used its magic to resurrect Osiris long enough to conceive an heir, a son named Horus, who later challenged Seth and became the pharaoh. Isis had her revenge, but she was afraid that Seth would retaliate by freeing the demons that lived in the chaos at the edge of the universe."

"Something worse than those animals we saw tonight?" Sara asked anxiously.

"Far worse," Sudi said. "Isis gave the Book of Thoth to the Hour priests and told them to watch the night skies. When the stars warned of danger, the priests were supposed to give the book to the pharaoh so he could use its magic to protect the world."

"But there aren't any pharaohs anymore," Sara said.

"Nowadays, the priests give the book to the next Descendants," Sudi explained.

"There must be zillions of people alive today who are related to the pharaohs," Brian argued.

"But only those born with the royal birthmark are the chosen Descendants," Sudi explained.

Sara gasped. "That weird mark under your hair—is it . . . ?"

"It's the sacred eye of Horus," Sudi said. "It's the reason I was summoned and not my sisters."

"Oh, my God," Sara muttered as she stared out

at the night. "My best friend is some kind of super-hero."

"Meri and Dalila are Descendants, too," Sudi added softly.

Brian let out a long hiss of air. "And the cult is devoted to Seth, and that's why you were summoned, to stop them."

"Yes," Sudi said. "They want to return the universe to chaos and bring Seth back as the supreme ruler."

"That day in the museum when you started reading the hieroglyphs on the mummy case," Sara said, "I thought you were teasing me, but you really can read them."

"That was around the time I was summoned," Sudi explained. "It was all new for me then, and scary. It still is."

"No wonder you're always over at Abdel's house." Sara thought for a moment. "He's an Hour priest, isn't he?"

"Yes, he's my guide," Sudi explained, her throat tight with anxiety. "But so far I think I've disappointed him. I haven't done a very good job."

"That's not true," Sara argued back. "What

would have happened to me tonight if you hadn't risked your life to save me?" She leaned against Sudi and squeezed her hand fiercely. "Thank you," she whispered before she started crying again.

This time, Sudi let her own tears fall, finally releasing the tension that had been building up inside her. By the time she had finished, Brian had parked the car in the alley behind her house.

Sara caught her arm before she climbed out. "Sudi, I'm sorry."

"About what?" Sudi asked.

"I should never have listened to Michelle," Sara explained. "I should have trusted my feelings and listened to you."

"It's all right," Sudi reassured her, grateful their friendship was on solid ground again.

"Friends forever?" Sara asked, holding out her pinkie. Sudi caught it, and they hooked their little fingers.

"Forever," Sudi answered. Then she let go and crawled out of the car.

As she slammed the door, she realized that Brian had gotten out, too. He walked over to her.

"What's with all the things that have been

happening to me?" he asked, all the bluster gone from his voice. "Like, the other night, I woke up from this really weird dream and found myself outside your house helping you crawl through a basement window."

"The goddess Isis uses you to help me, and I'm glad she does," Sudi explained, "because every time you've shown up, you've rescued me."

"Sweet damn," he said. "Out of all the girls in D.C., you were the one who was chosen."

"Brian," Sudi whined. "Please don't start. I already know I'm not good enough, and I don't need you to remind me."

He put his arms around her. "You sacrificed your life tonight to save both me and Sara. In my book, that makes you the right choice and good enough." He pulled back. "Dang, and I'm playing a part in this."

"Yes." She nodded.

"Cool," he sauntered back to the driver's side, his swagger returning.

"You can't tell anyone," she said.

"Do I look like an idiot?" he asked, then he caught her look. "I know that's what you think, but

I'm going to show you. I've waited my whole life for an adventure like this."

"I'm sure that's why Isis chose you," Sudi said softly, but she also knew it was because Brian was fearless and never faltered. He always came through, no matter what the danger was. "You were the one who really saved Sara tonight," Sudi added. "If you hadn't come out of the trance and distracted all those cult members, I don't know what would have happened."

He smiled broadly. "Catch you later." He waved and got back into his seat behind the steering wheel.

Sudi waited until the car drove away; then she hurried across the yard. She still had one more thing she needed to do.

The aroma of coffee hit her as soon as she stepped inside the house. She froze. The night had passed, and her parents were already in the kitchen having breakfast before the morning sun. How was she going to explain the way she looked to them? No way she could blame it on street hockey this time.

CHAPTER 17

Reluctantly, Sudi stepped out of her muddy shoes and went into the kitchen to face her parents.

"What are you doing up so early?" her mother asked, folding the newspaper down. Their eyes met, and her mother gawked at her. "Sudi?"

Her father spilled his coffee as he set his cup down. "What happened to you?"

Without waiting for an answer, her mother pushed back her chair and rushed over to her. She rolled the shredded sleeve up and examined the cuts on Sudi's arm.

At once, Sudi grasped the truth. Her parents' trust in her was so strong that they had never considered the possibility that she was just getting home from a night out with friends. They thought she had gotten up early and gone outside.

Sudi slowly started her lie. "I went jogging—"

"—And took one heck of a fall," her father added. "You're lucky you didn't break your arm."

"I'm not sure what cut me," Sudi said, embellishing her lie. "My sweatshirt was caught on something that pulled my arm one way while my body was skidding in the opposite direction over this incredibly foul mud."

"You have to be more careful," her father chided gently.

"Take a shower and put bandages over these cuts," her mother said as new worry filled her eyes. "Promise me you won't go running alone. What if something worse had happened? We wouldn't have known where you were, or how to find you."

Sudi felt ashamed that she had lied to them when they so firmly trusted her. She watched them go back to their newspapers and coffee before she left the kitchen.

Moments later, in her sisters' room, Sudi nudged Carrie. "Wake up."

"It's Saturday," Carrie said as she snuggled down under the covers. "And get out of here; you stink."

Patty Pie lay on the bed between Sudi's twin sisters. The yellow cat opened one eye, his nose crinkling to take in the forest scent clinging to Sudi before he stretched luxuriously.

Sudi lifted the covers. "The ghost wants to possess my body."

Carrie jackknifed into a sitting position and shook Nicole.

"The ghost is trying to possess Sudi," Carrie said.

Sleepily, Nicole sat up and threw the covers aside. "We warned you." Nicole glanced around the room. "The ghost isn't in the room yet." Her tone implied that she would be soon.

"We'll get rid of the ghost. Don't worry." Carrie hugged Sudi in spite of the mud covering her clothes. Then Nicole came around the bed and joined the sister-hug, her hair smelling of strawberry shampoo.

"How can you be sure?" Sudi asked, remembering the ghost's promise.

Suddenly, Pie yowled and arched his back. The cat hissed, then jumped off the bed and raced under the desk.

"What scared him?" Sudi asked.

Her sisters grabbed her hands and pulled her down on the carpet, forming a circle of three as the bedroom door flew open and banged against the wall. The ghost rushed into the room and whirled around Sudi's head. After she had tangled her hair, she took on the translucent form of a woman.

Nicole and Carrie began reciting words in a language that Sudi didn't understand.

"You will not make me leave," the ghost said and flew up.

In response, Sudi's sisters spoke more rapidly.

Outraged by their defiance, the ghost knocked Nicole's china-doll collection off the shelf. Pieces of the white ceramic faces spun through the air. Sudi ducked but never let go of her sisters' hands.

Rotating violently, the ghost lifted the bedspread, twisting it up to the ceiling. Then, unexpectedly, she vanished. The bedspread fell and hit the floor with a soft thud.

"You got rid of her." Sudi looked around. "Thank you."

"We didn't finish the necessary rites." Carrie surveyed the room.

"But everything is quiet now," Sudi said, not sharing her sisters' misgivings. "And I saw the ghost disappear."

Nicole picked up two pieces of fragile china and tried to fit them back together to form a face. "We didn't make the ghost leave," she said quietly. "She'll be back."

"What in blazes are you girls doing?" Their father shouted from the hallway. His feet pounded on the carpet. He entered the room, shaking his head. "Your room looks like a pigsty. How in tarnation did you do this?"

Sudi jumped up. "It's my fault. I got lightheaded, and when I started to fall I grabbed on to the shelf. Look what I did to Nicole's china-doll collection."

Carrie joined in. "We tried to catch her, but she's bigger and—"

Their father held up his hand. "Are they telling the truth, Nicole?"

Nicole threw the shattered doll face across the room and looked ready to cry. "Yeah," she said at last.

Sudi placed her arms around her sisters, overwhelmed with gratitude. "I'm going to use the money in my bank account to replace the dolls. That's a solemn promise."

Nicole let the tears fall down her cheeks. "Thanks, Sudi."

Their father looked both surprised and proud. "That's very generous of you."

"No, it's not," Sudi muttered, and without looking back, she walked to her room, leaving her sisters to clean up the mess. Her body ached all over, and she fell across her bed, not caring about the mud on her clothes.

CHAPTER 18

By Monday afternoon, Sudi's optimism had returned. Zack and his friends hadn't bothered her all day. And soon she would be able to tell Dalila, Meri, and Abdel everything that had happened on Friday night. With the information she had now, she felt certain that Abdel would be able to help her find a way to release Zack from his membership in the cult.

Even though she was feeling confident, the ghost's threat had made her realize that something bad could happen to her, and if it did, she wanted her parents and sisters to know how much she cared for them. So on Sunday she had written a long letter to each of them and hidden the letters in her underwear drawer, where they would be found after her death.

Now she opened her locker. When she caught her reflection in the mirror, she was surprised that her eyes didn't look tired. Several times that day she'd had a peculiar sensation that the classroom was whirling around her. The dizziness seemed to come and go, along with blurred vision, and always left her feeling oddly devoid of energy.

She tossed her geometry book in and then, closing her locker, turned and bumped into Raul. "Were you standing behind me the whole time?" she asked, wondering why she hadn't seen his reflection in the mirror.

"Yes, I even said hello, but you were so lost in thought you didn't hear me," Raul said. "Do you want to tell me what's on your mind?"

She shrugged. "Nothing to tell, really, I'm just feeling tired."

He looked disappointed. "I was hoping you'd go out with me tonight."

"It's a school night," she teased.

"I need to see you." He slipped his arm around her. For a moment she thought he was going to overcome his shyness and kiss her, right there in front of everyone.

And then he did.

The sensation of his soft lips touching hers was more pleasant than any of her fantasies. When he pulled back, she sighed. She liked the way he made her feel, all butterflies and sweet ache. She glanced up at him and wondered if she was falling in love. She had had many crushes, but the feelings inside her now were different. Her boundaries were falling down, and as she stared into his eyes, she wondered if he would be the one.

Seeming to sense her feelings, he whispered, "I feel the same way about you. You're my first love."

She felt herself blush.

He smiled in response.

"Hey!" Sara interrupted them. "Art class tonight," she reminded Sudi, and then she smiled knowingly. "But I imagine you can't come with me. You probably have lots you need to tell Abdel."

"Call me," Sudi said to Raul. After a quick

good-bye and a short hug, she walked outside with Sara.

"How did your day go?" Sudi asked.

"Great!" Sara said with a mischievous grin. "Every time some girl asked me about my date with Zack, I told her, all confidentially, like she was the only one I was going to tell, that when he kissed me it was like licking the bottom of a snail."

"Yuck," Sudi groaned. "That's disgusting."

"I know," Sara said, enjoying herself. "But I don't want any other girl to date him and find herself forced into joining the cult, so, if you hear stories about his terrible problems with nasal congestion, you'll know who started the rumor."

"You're bad," Sudi said, delighted.

"I know," Sara grinned. "Aren't you glad I'm on your side?"

Sudi hugged her as they strolled down the walkway in the glaring winter sunshine.

Zack, Garrett, and Nick were waiting near the curb. When they saw Sudi, they walked toward her, staring at her feet. Zack stopped, the wind lifting the tail of his black coat, and said something to the others.

Nick and Garrett started laughing.

Sudi glanced down. "What's making them laugh?" When she looked up again, she didn't like the apprehension she saw on Sara's face.

"Walk," Sara said, looking panicked.

"Why?"

"Just do it!" Sara squealed, staring down at Sudi's feet.

Alarmed, Sudi took a step forward.

"You don't have a shadow," Sara said, starting to hyperventilate.

"That's not possible," Sudi said.

"Look down!" Sara gasped.

Sudi did. There was no dark patch beneath her feet. She glanced up at the sun to make sure something wasn't blocking the source of light. Her body was definitely between the sun's rays and the sidewalk, yet she cast no shadow. It was as if the sunlight shone through her. Her heart lurched, and when the beat came back, it was painfully fast. How had Zack and his friends stolen her shadow, and, even more important, what did it mean?

CHAPTER 19

"I wish you would have told me sooner." Abdel looked distressed when Sudi finished recounting everything that had happened on Friday night and before. "Why do you lack confidence in me?"

His reaction surprised her. She had thought he'd be angry with her. Instead, he was blaming himself for what had happened.

"It was my mistake," Sudi said. "I knew it was wrong to steal the bracelet. You can't blame yourself for that."

He continued pacing back and forth in the room where he stored the Book of Thoth and other sacred texts. "I'm the one who failed," he said, "because you should have come to me first when you saw the ghost, and yet you didn't. I'm supposed to be your mentor, the one you rely on when things become difficult."

Sudi stared down at the table. "But if I'd told you about the ghost, then I would have had to tell you about the bracelet I'd stolen, and you would have gone all hyper on me."

"Hyper?" He turned quickly, the sudden movement causing the flames inside the oil-filled bowls to flicker close to the wall. Streams of soot blackened the white paint. "What do you mean, 'hyper'?"

"Like you're acting now," Meri butted in. "Sudi did exactly what I would have done. You expect us to be perfect, but how can we be when we're still learning? It's not like we grew up knowing about ghosts and demons."

"Besides, who wouldn't want a pet ghost?" Dalila asked. "Sudi said the ghost was really nice and funny until she talked to the cult leader."

"Even then, she only turned on me after she thought I had deceived her," Sudi added.

Abdel tried to smile, but he remained distraught. He sat down at the table next to Sudi, his expression gentle. "Next time you encounter a supernatural entity, tell me about it before you decide to make it your pet. You must develop trust in me, because I can assure you that having your shadow stolen from you will not be the worst thing that happens to you as a Descendant."

"If that was supposed to comfort her," Meri said, "I know it didn't. You even gave *me* the willies. I mean, what can be worse than having someone take your shadow? How's she supposed to go outside when the sun is shining? People are going to notice."

"Why is my shadow missing?" Sudi asked.

"The ancient Egyptians believed that a person's shadow was actually a part of the person," Dalila explained. "So stealing your shadow is like stealing a part of you."

Abdel nodded in agreement. "The shadow was seen as both a part of its owner and something that had a separate existence."

Sudi shuddered. "I always just took it for granted that it was a result of my body blocking the light, but if it's really part of me, like an arm or a leg or a soul, then I want it back."

"We'll get it back," Abdel said. "Your shadow is especially important in the afterlife. I suppose that you could say that it's a manner of continuation after death."

"You mean, like, one of my dead relatives could send their shadow to check on me?" Meri looked worried.

"Let's stay on the problem at hand," Abdel said. "Having Sudi's shadow taken from her is the first step in possessing her body. It's actually an old magician's trick, very theatrical, to weaken an opponent's fighting spirit and make him an easier victim."

"It's working," Sudi said miserably.

"We don't have to worry until you see the ghost's shadow at your feet rather than your own. That won't happen until its *ka*, its being, is inside you. Then it will control your body, but the possession still won't be complete until—"

"You're scaring her," Meri interrupted and rubbed Sudi's back.

"Don't worry." Dalila walked over to the shelves that held the copper chests. She picked out one and brought it back to the table, then pulled out a cylindrical leather case. "Some of the curses in the Execration Texts can be used to exorcise malignant ghosts."

Abdel had been watching her with curiosity, and now he spoke. "I believe this situation is far more complicated than reciting a simple spell."

"You do?" Dalila set the case aside. Her eyes expressed concern now as she concentrated on Abdel.

"I'm certain that the spirit Sudi brought back when she stole the bracelet is really a *mut*, one of the dangerous dead."

Sudi looked up. "How is that different from a regular ghost?"

"Sometimes, when a person dies violently, he can become an unsettled spirit. That is the kind that we are most familiar with," Abdel said, "the type that haunts a house. But the dangerous dead are malevolent spirits who refuse to pass on to the realm of the dead. In life, they were treacherous and dedicated to evil, and in death they are even more so. Their souls remain earthbound, only because they will it so."

"But the ghost didn't seem evil to Sudi," Dalila reminded him.

"She would have been trying to seduce her and make her lose caution," he explained. "I'm confident that she has been siphoning off Sudi's power without her even being aware, and that this is the reason Sudi has been unable to use her wand."

Dalila looked stricken. "You mean, the spirit has been using Sudi's power to destroy the cosmic harmony?"

"As she gains Sudi's power in the present," Abdel explained, "the likelihood grows that it will be able to return to the past and, from that vantage point in time, destroy the universe and start over with the god Seth as king. The power within Sudi, when combined with that of her wand, is able to move the stars."

"You said that the stars are already moving," Meri said, "but the newscast this morning said that the way the stars were clustering was an optical illusion, a distortion caused by gases from solar flares."

"What else can they say?" Sudi asked. "They certainly can't blame magic."

"The constellation Sahu is changing position," Abdel explained. "But worse, Ikhemu-seku, the stars that never fail, have started to move."

"We saw that this weekend," Dalila said. "I can't believe that the scientists don't know the truth. They must see other evidence of dark energies causing the universe to contract."

"Once the *mut* has stolen all the power within you," Abdel went on, staring at Sudi, "then, I'm confident that it will steal your wand and return with it to the past."

"In my body?" Sudi asked.

Abdel nodded. "And complete what it has already begun."

"The destruction of the universe," Dalila said, with a mixture of defeat and terror on her face.

The room suddenly felt too closed, the smoke too heavy to breathe. "I did this?" Sudi asked in a small, strained voice.

"Not knowingly," Abdel said. Then he frowned. "What puzzles me is why the spirit wants to possess your body."

"Maybe she needs to use her hands to carry the wand back to the past," Meri said.

"That's a possibility," Abdel said. "But she could do that as a spirit also."

"Sudi watched the ghost lift Sara's hair and empty Michelle's purse," Dalila explained. "So the ghost can obviously levitate things. She must have another reason for wanting to possess Sudi."

"But what could it be?" Sudi asked.

"Why would the spirit want to be hampered by the physical restraints that a mortal body imposes?" Abdel asked, staring at Sudi.

"I'm sorry." Sudi looked at her friends. Abdel had told her that Descendants who failed were condemned to live with the demons in the chaos at the edge of the universe. She didn't want Meri and Dalila to suffer that fate because of her stupidity.

Meri clasped Sudi's hand. "It's all right. You didn't do anything that I wouldn't have done."

"Besides, the ancient Egyptians had spells to protect themselves from apparitions," Dalila said, too cheerily. "I'll find one that will work in your situation and give it to you." She glanced at Abdel. "Unless you have a different plan."

"We need to stop the spirit before it takes over Sudi's body," Abdel said. "And for now, the best we have are the curses in the Execration Texts."

"What will happen to the ghost?" Sudi asked.

"She will be punished," Abdel replied.

"A damned soul's punishment continues into the afterlife," Dalila added.

Sudi had seen paintings depicting the tortures of the damned. "Isn't there another way?" she asked. "As much as I feel afraid of the spirit now, I still don't think she deserves that kind of punishment. The ghost wasn't evil until the cult captured her, and it's my fault that she was captured in the first place."

"But you must consider this," Abdel said sternly. "It's very possible that the spirit is trying to arouse your sympathy. If you pity her, and believe that she is the victim, then you will be less likely to attack her or deliver her harm in any way."

"He's right," Meri said. "If you feel sorry for her and feel like you're responsible for what has happened to her, then you'll want to help her."

"And while you're trying to help her, she could destroy you," Dalila concluded.

"But I just can't believe she's one of the dangerous dead," Sudi said.

Abdel sighed wearily. "Arguing with me isn't going to solve the problem. We have to take action. We have no other choice."

Sudi stood.

"Everything is going to be all right," Meri tried to reassure her.

"We'll stop the ghost," Dalila said. "It's like Abdel said: this won't be the worst thing that we have to face."

"But it could be the last," Sudi grumbled. "I just need some time alone."

She raced down the stairs and outside. Then, glancing up at the night sky, she started walking, studying the clustered stars. She headed around the corner and bumped into Zack. Her self-control broke.

"Stop following me," she said and shoved him hard. "I have enough problems without you and your stupid bullying."

His hands flew up, and for a moment she thought he was going to shove her back. Instead, he grabbed her shoulders and kissed her.

CHAPTER 20

"I love you," Zack said.

The words stunned Sudi. For a moment she wondered if she had heard him correctly. She stopped struggling and brushed back her hair. "Love me?" she asked. "You've been following me and making my life miserable."

Even in the dim light she could see the hurt on his face. "I didn't mean to make you miserable."

"Well, you did." She turned and walked away from him. Windblown trash skittered across her path.

In front of a restaurant he caught her arm and pulled her back to him. The door opened as a couple stepped outside. Heat and the smells of grilling onions escaped into the cold air.

"I was trying to get you alone so I could tell you how I feel about you," he said. "I guess I screwed up."

"Deeply," she added. "Next time use your cell phone and come out with it." She scanned the shadows at the edge of the building, expecting cult members to round the corner any moment and kidnap her.

"Listen to me," Zack pleaded.

"Here's a clue," Sudi said. "If you like a girl, treat her nice. You don't push her off a building."

"It was never my intention to hurt you," he assured her.

"I'm supposed to believe you?" She turned away, stuffing her gloved hands into her pockets to protect them from the bitter cold. Her face stung as she walked quickly into the brisk wind.

"I needed to see you transform," he explained, catching up to her again. "That night at the Tidal Basin, a magnificent bird flew over the water. My friends told me that it must be you. I had to see for myself. When I saw your wings—" He stopped, seemingly spellbound by the memory, "I was overwhelmed with love."

He caught the back of her coat and tenderly pulled her into his arms. Sudi didn't resist this time. His body felt warm, and she couldn't leave him until she had the answers she needed.

"I've loved you from the time we were in elementary school. I used to chase you around with bugs just to get your attention."

"I didn't know," was all she could think to say.

"How could you have known?" he asked. "You always thought of me as just your friend. Do you know how much it hurt when you talked to me about the other guys?"

"But my stories always made you laugh," she argued.

"Each one broke my heart," he whispered.

"You never let on," she said, still staggered by what he was telling her. "I wish you had told me before now."

"With so many guys liking you, what chance did I have?" he asked. "You're amazingly beautiful and popular. But then last year some guys in the cult told me that the cult leader could grant any wish."

Distraught, she said, "So you joined the cult."

"To have you." He smiled down at her.

She wondered why she hadn't noticed how incredibly handsome he was before now. He was drop-dead gorgeous, just like all the girls at school said, but she had always seen him as just her reliable friend. She blinked and tried to pull her eyes away from his gaze.

"You said they forced you to join the cult," she reminded him.

"I didn't understand that all of this was real," he said. "I went out to the woods thinking I was going to a beer party."

"So they tricked you, the same way you tried to trick Sara," she said.

He nodded. "When the priest touched my head, I felt—"

"He took your soul," she concluded.

"My life changed," he went on. "Everything had such clarity after he spoke the incantation over me."

"Is your soul kept in a canopic jar like the ones I saw Friday night?" she asked.

"Maybe," he said. "Why are you concerned about that?"

"Because I'll find a way to steal your soul back and free you," she promised.

"Free me from what?" He looked puzzled. "I'm not imprisoned or held against my will. I have more freedom now than you do with all your rules. I make my own, change them, forget them. I live my life free."

"That's a delusion," she snapped back.

"You're the one who's being deceived and misled." His eyes were so serious that for a moment she believed him. Then the wretched feeling returned, and she became heavyhearted again; this was all her fault. "Don't you want your soul back, Zack?"

"You don't understand. Hell is a dark paradise," he said with rising excitement. "Let me show you another way of living."

"Never," she said, shaking her head. "I couldn't."

"You think it will be bad because you only know one way. Let me reveal the unknown to you."

She took a deep breath and stepped away from him. She had almost said yes. What was he doing to her? Terrified, she started walking. Wind raced through the denuded branches overhead, spilling strange shadows across the sidewalk in front of her.

"I can feel your attraction to the darkness," he said, striding beside her. "Just say yes, and then I can tell you the secret that Abdel is keeping from you."

"Abdel?" She stopped, surprised. "What secret?" And then she caught herself. "Abdel would never keep anything from me."

"Why do you trust him when you barely know him?" Zack asked indignantly. "He even used deception when he summoned you."

Part of her wanted to trust Zack, but how could she, when he belonged to the cult? Then another thought intruded. "Did you know I was—?"

"A Descendant?" he finished her sentence for her. "No. I found out later that the cult was planning to destroy you and your friends, but the high priest promised me that he would find a way for me to have you, because he knew that our love—"

"Your love," she said, correcting him.

He ignored her. "He knew that our love was the forever kind."

"No, Zack. That's not what I feel."

"Give our love a chance," he said. "Promise me that you'll stop going out with other guys. I'll be patient. You don't have to do anything yet. I'll wait until you love me."

She stiffened and drew back. "We're just friends, Zack. That's all we'll ever be." There was no doubt in her mind.

She saw the muscles in his jaw tighten.

"I can't force myself to love you, Zack," she explained.

He smiled coldly. "Don't you understand my power?" he asked. "That alone should make you want me."

Before she could answer, his arm swept down. A violent gust rushed around them. The branches overhead cracked as the tree toppled and hit the street with a loud thwack.

"Did you do that?" she asked, not quite believing that he had. A tree falling could have been an odd coincidence on this windy night.

"Believe in me," he whispered when he sensed

her doubt. He lifted his hand again. The air filled with a curious crackling sound, and then the tree burst into flames.

Sudi cried out and jumped back, away from the sudden heat.

The noise and fire brought people running outside from the restaurant and the drugstore on the corner. People were already calling 911 on their cell phones.

"Oh, Zack," Sudi said mournfully. Instead of hating him, she felt sorry for him and blamed herself. Somehow she should have sensed how desperately he was hurting. If she hadn't been so self-centered, then maybe she could have stopped him before he surrendered his life to the cult.

"I promise I'll save you," she said, staring into the blaze.

Within the smoke, she smelled the stinging scent of Zack's aftershave. The fragrance surprised her, because she hadn't smelled it on him when he was holding her. She turned to look at him, but he was gone. A sleek black animal, like the creatures she had seen in the forest out in Virginia, ran away from her. Without any doubt, the scent she had been breathing was that of conjured magic, not aftershave.

She staggered back, dumbfounded. The cult had done more to Zack than take his soul.

CHAPTER 21

By the time Sudi made her way into CVS, fire engines were rumbling down the street outside. She grabbed a bag of lollipops, then stood in line and used her cell phone to call Meri.

Trying to calm herself, she drew in a deep breath, but when Meri answered she still couldn't speak. She was trembling so violently that people in the store had stopped what they were doing to stare at her.

"What's wrong?" Meri asked.

"Zack followed me after I left Abdel's," Sudi said finally, sounding as if she had a cold. Her nose was still congested with smoke and the residue from Zack's magic. "I'm going home." Sudi stifled a sob. "Just come over when you're finished there. I don't want to be alone tonight."

She hung up, and immediately Meri called back. "Are you all right?"

"I'm safe." Sudi answered. "But I can't talk, because everyone in the store is watching me."

The stop-action that had held the customers and salesclerks suddenly released them. They turned away from Sudi and went about their business. The cashier called for the next in line.

Sudi barged ahead, out of turn, and slammed the bag of candy on the counter. After paying, she tore open the cellophane, took out a yellow sucker, and, leaving the rest, hurried outside.

Striding through the smoke-filled air, she licked the lemon-flavored sweet before putting it in her mouth. Years ago, when she had broken her arm at baseball camp, the coach had given her a lollipop to suck on, saying the sugar would keep her from going into shock. Sudi didn't know if that had been true or not, but right now the candy was definitely keeping her from bawling.

Police cars had blocked off the street. She darted through the barricades, skipping over the fire hoses, and broke into a run as a sudden gust whipped red cinders and ash around her.

Less than ten minutes later, she entered her house and leaned against the door. Heat encircled her, and with the warmth, her muscles began to relax.

Still brooding over everything that had happened, she took off her coat, gloves, and scarf, then started up the stairs. The soft clicking of computer keys came from her parents' room. She crept past the open doorway.

Her mother glanced up from her laptop. "Hi, Sudi. How was—" Her smile faded, replaced by a look of alarm. "What's wrong?"

"I didn't do too well on the geometry test today," Sudi lied, hurrying down the hall. "I better go to my room and start studying for the next one."

She could hear her mother getting up and walking behind her.

"You've never cried over a test," her mother

said. The flowery scent of her perfume and the aroma of her coffee accompanied her into the room. She still had on her black business suit, but she had taken off her high heels and was wearing fluffy pink slippers.

"I guess there's always a first time," Sudi said.

"I want to talk to you about your low mood," her mother began, tapping her finger on the cup she held in her hands.

"Mom, there's nothing to talk about." Sudi had meant for the words to come out with confidence, to dispel her mother's concern. Instead, anguish filled her voice.

"You seem more than a little down," her mother said cautiously, setting her cup of coffee on the nightstand.

Sudi snorted.

"Maybe we should talk." Her mother sat on the edge of the bed and crossed her legs.

Sudi wanted to fall into her mother's arms and tell her everything. But she couldn't. "Mom, I don't want to hear another lecture about the dark before the dawn. I'm glad you're concerned and all, but this time you're not going to be able to change what's happening to me with encouraging words."

Rather than argue, her mother smiled. "This won't be a standard lecture. I want to tell you something about me when I was young."

Sudi glanced at her clock. She didn't have time for this.

"I had these fits of despair like I see you going through now."

"It's not despair," Sudi said, correcting her.

"If it's not despair, then maybe there's something you're keeping from me that we should talk about," her mother said firmly.

Sudi chewed on the inside of her mouth, trying to decide whether she should tell her mother the truth. After all, Sara and Brian had believed her. Maybe her mother would, too. For a moment she imagined her mother going to the police and exposing the cult, but the daydream quickly ended. What good would that do? Only the Descendants had the power to use the magic in the Book of Thoth, and there was no other way to fight the cult. Military weapons, no matter how powerful, couldn't defeat incantations and sorcery.

"All right, I'm miserable," Sudi confessed.

Her mother cuddled her and held her tight. "The first time it happened to me, I thought I would never be able to escape it, but after I'd gone through a few episodes, I realized that the sorrow was my way of saying good-bye to my old self."

Sudi stared at the floor and waited for her mother to go on.

"For me, a change in who I am is always preceded by deep, horrible sadness," her mother explained. "Poets call it walking eyeball deep through hell, and movie stars call it reinventing themselves."

Sudi considered what her mother was saying. Maybe this misery and hating what her life had become was part of the journey, the metamorphosis into becoming a Descendant. She definitely needed to change. She couldn't live this way, always cowering, waiting in fear for the next demon to show up.

"Maybe your soul knows it's time to move on and challenge yourself with something new," her mother said. "I know you must feel afraid, too, because change also means giving up the comfort of the life you've become used to. Maybe that's the hardest part."

Sudi nodded. She definitely didn't want to give

up the fun she had had as a party girl. It was hard to shift from that identity to superhero, defender of the world. She sighed, and her mother squeezed her hand. Perhaps it was time, as her mother said, to move on and become a true Descendant. She had to stop living with the false hope that Abdel would realize he'd made a mistake when he'd summoned her, and call forth someone else.

"I think that's what you're struggling with, even if you see it as a problem outside yourself that's making you unhappy." Her mother stood and picked up her cup of coffee. "Change is what life's all about." Then she added with a laugh, "That's the only thing that is constant."

Sudi jumped up and hugged her mother. "Thanks, Mom."

At the door, her mother turned back. "Comfort has a terrible price, Sudi. I don't want you to let your life go unlived because you're afraid of change. Too many people do, and then at the end, what do they have to look back on?"

After her mother left the room, Sudi took her wand from the closet wall, where she had taped it. She smoothed her hand over the bronze surface, then stood with it in front of her mirror, trying to imagine herself as the defender of the world.

"You're a superhero," she said, endeavoring to fit the title to her frazzled-looking face.

Still gazing at her reflection, she said, "You are the divine sister of the goddess Isis."

In response, sparks flew from the tip of the wand, startling her. The tiny white stars fell across her face, tickling and sparkling, before vanishing.

Overjoyed, she whooped exuberantly as power rose inside her.

"Sudi," her mother called from the other room. "Is everything all right?"

"Never been better, Mom," Sudi answered.

A naughty grin crossed her face. She had memorized several incantations for beauty. Did she dare use one now?

Without thinking more, she intoned, "Beloved goddess Isis, speaker of spells, I entreat you, share your magic with me. As the moon rides high each night, let its light bathe me in beauty."

A milky glow shone through her window. Sudi took in a sharp breath as her face became suffused with lunar light. Her hair rose, curling up and out, then settled, glossy and sleek, over her shoulders. At the same time, her eyes became sultry, as if she had spent hours brushing mascara over the lashes and lining the lids with soft gray color.

For the first time since becoming a Descendant, fear wasn't clouding her thoughts—and why should she have been afraid? The goddess Isis had given her the secrets of the universe to learn and use wisely. She could even feel the change in her wand. It began vibrating, replicating her newfound strength.

She left her room, determined to face Zack. She was going to convince him to help her stop the ghost and get her power back. They had once been best friends, and he claimed he loved her, so why wouldn't he help her? Her confidence swelled. Tonight the stars would return to their correct positions in the night sky.

"I'm going over to Zack's house to study," she yelled as she bounded down the stairs to get her wool coat.

"Are you really?" her mother called after her.

"Yeah!" Sudi shouted. "I'm going to ace geometry. It's a lot better than walking through hell."

CHAPTER 22

Jagged bolts of lightning stitched through the clouds. The wind had changed direction, and the air had turned warm. Sudi stopped on the front lawn of the huge Victorian house, trying to remember what her father had told her. Warm, humid currents pushing in from the Atlantic Ocean sometimes mixed with winterlike systems and set off powerful thunderstorms over D.C. Foul weather could ruin what she had planned to have Zack help her do.

She hurried across the porch and rang the doorbell.

Zack's sister, Brenda, opened the front door. Her black hair, unkempt, was spritzed and sprayed to stay that way. She had been rubbing her eyes, and her false lashes were coming undone.

"What's with the snake head?" Brenda asked as Sudi stepped inside. "Did you join that creepy cult, too?"

"No," Sudi answered, making a mental note to come back some day and talk to Brenda. She was the first person, so far, that Sudi had heard call the cult creepy. "Is Zack home?"

"He's in his room," Brenda said, already turning back to the music blaring from the front room. "Go on up."

Distant thunder rolled lazily through the night as Sudi ran up the stairs. Two years before, Zack's parents had renovated the attic and given him the entire floor. Sudi had helped him pick out the chairs, paint the walls, and arrange his bookshelves.

Quietly, she pushed the door open to a second stairwell, then crept up the steps. Near the top, she peeked through the bars that supported the handrail bordering the stairs on the open side of the room.

Zack was sprawled out on his bed, bare-chested, wearing baggy shorts. The ceiling fans were turned on, and the rotating blades made shadows flicker over him.

He jumped up when he saw her and rushed to her. "Sudi."

"Zack, I came here because—"

He pressed a finger over her lips. "I'm glad you're here. You don't have to make up an excuse to come see me."

While Zack helped her take off her coat, she tried to refocus her thoughts so she could tell him her plan and convince him to help her.

He took her wand and coat and placed both on a green beanbag chair. When he came back to her, she said, "I need to talk to you because—"

"You don't need to say the words." He gently cupped her face between his hands and surprised her with a kiss. When he pulled back, he added, "You wouldn't be here unless you had come to tell me that you've changed your mind and you're going to try."

"That's not why I'm here, Zack," she said, feeling confused. She shouldn't have enjoyed his kiss, and yet she had. And even more baffling to her was her sudden desire to forget the reason for her visit and fall into his embrace. Dumbfounded, she stared at his arm, the rock-hard muscles under his tanned skin.

"Why did you come here?" he asked gently, rousing her from her thoughts.

"We need to have a long talk," she said, trying to remember her plan. It had been so clear in her mind before. Was he doing something to her?

"About what?" he asked.

"If you'll help me," she stated at last, "then I'm pretty sure we can stop the cult and save you."

He laughed. "You don't need to save me. I've explained that already." He smoothed his hands down her sides, then pulled her against his chest. "Stop being coy. You put on makeup and your hair looks gorgeous. You didn't do that just to come over to *talk* to me or tell me about some plan. I know better; I felt your reaction to my kiss."

Sudi groaned. Her spell to make herself look beautiful had backfired.

"I'm glad you changed your mind," he whispered

against her ear, his breath warm and sweet.

"We've always been just good friends, Zack," Sudi said, pulling back. "Isn't that enough?"

"It's never been enough for me." He worked his fingers around her waist, pulling her closer. "And I don't think it's enough for you, either. Girls at school are crushing on me. Some even give me notes or call me. They don't even know me and they want to hook up. But you're the one I've chosen."

"Even if I cared for you the way you want me to, Zack, what could I do? We're enemies."

"You could love me in spite of that," he continued. "I know you could. That's all you have to say, that you'll defy Isis and the Hour priests to be with me."

The sadness in his eyes almost made her want to try. "But friendship is all it's ever going to be," she said, wondering why *she* felt disappointed.

His expression changed. "No," he said firmly. "Not anymore."

His sudden anger surprised her, and she snapped to attention. "What do you mean *not anymore*?"

"The cult gave you to me," he said.

"Seriously, you can't believe that," Sudi said. "They can't just give a person to you."

The ghost appeared beside them, her gossamer shape fluttering in the breeze from the ceiling fan. Suddenly, Sudi understood their plan.

"As soon as the ghost takes over your body, then you'll be mine," Zack announced.

"But it won't be me," Sudi argued. "Don't do this, Zack."

He lifted his hand, and the ghost rushed toward Sudi. Her vision clouded as the ghost's *ka*, its supernatural essence, entered her. She blinked. She could still see, although only hazily.

This time, when Zack leaned down to kiss her, she had no control over her body's response. Still, the intensity of her desire for Zack surprised her.

"It's been so long since I've felt a lover's embrace," the ghost breathed, using Sudi's voice.

Now that Sudi shared the same body with the ghost, she was able to read her thoughts and see her memories as if they were her own. The ghost hadn't stolen Sudi's power. She didn't want to destroy the world. She just wanted to make her way to the land of the dead—to spend a happy eternity in the Field of Rushes.

With sudden startling clarity, Sudi realized something else. The ghost and Zack were a distraction. The cult had used them both to keep Sudi off balance. But if the ghost wasn't the real threat, then who or what was?

Abruptly she remembered the message that Isis had given her through Brian that night outside her house. *Matter is nothing more than a manifestation of energy.* Suddenly, a lot of things made sense to her, and she knew who the real enemy was. But how could she warn Dalila and Meri when she was trapped inside her own body?

Another kiss jolted her from her thoughts, this one more passionate than the others.

"I love you, Sudi," Zack whispered as he eased her toward his bed.

CHAPTER 23

Sudi opened her eyes, surprised to find herself still standing in the center of Zack's attic loft. She must have temporarily lost consciousness, because Dalila and Meri stood protectively in front of her now, the tips of their wands pressed against her heart.

"Whoa," Sudi said, feeling woozy and completely strange.

Something bobbled inside her chest, a curious sensation, like liquid sloshing back and forth against her rib cage.

"You're all right." Meri grabbed her arm to steady her. "That's just the ghost inside you fighting Dalila's magic. She doesn't want to give up your body."

Her eyes half closed, Dalila appeared deep in concentration. Her lips were moving, and Sudi quickly realized that she was muttering curses from the Execration Texts.

When Dalila's eyes flashed open, the muscles across Sudi's shoulders twitched. A violent jerk followed as the spirit left her body; her see-through form twisted around Sudi's head. Then, shrieking, she whipped up past the ceiling fan and disappeared.

"You didn't hurt the ghost, did you?" Sudi asked, her words bumping out over gasps and wheezes as her lungs labored to regain their normal breathing pattern again.

"I can't believe you're concerned about the ghost." Meri gently rubbed Sudi's neck, trying to calm her.

"She didn't do anything wrong." Sudi flinched as her muscles cramped. "She was deceived by the cult." Without warning, the soreness in her shoulders grew, and new pain shot down her spine.

Meri braced herself against Sudi to keep her from falling. Quickly, Dalila placed her hands over the throbbing muscles and chanted a spell.

"I'm sorry," Dalila said. "I know it hurts. I had to use exceedingly potent magic to make the spirit leave your body. With that much negative energy floating inside of you, some of it was bound to affect you, but the pain should go away in a few seconds."

"Hopefully," Sudi groaned. "But you didn't send the spirit to eternal suffering, did you?"

"No," Dalila answered. "She left your body before I could."

Moments later, just as Dalila had predicted, the discomfort went away, and Sudi stood up straighter.

"The ghost definitely didn't want to give your body up," Meri said, and then she added with a grin, "I think it was smitten with Zack and having too much fun kissing him."

"Did you see?" Sudi asked.

"By the time we arrived, Zack was frantically

trying to work a counterspell to get the ghost to leave you," Dalila explained.

"He was?" Sudi asked, suddenly aware of the scent of Zack's magic permeating the air.

"Of course, he didn't have the right incantation," Dalila continued. "Curses are needed in a case like this, along with spells." She neatly folded up the papers on which she had copied the curses and slipped them into the pocket of her jeans.

"Zack is going to be in deep trouble when the cult leaders find out that he defied them," Meri said in a low voice. "You should have seen him try to help you. He was petrified that he was going to lose you."

"Where is he?" Sudi asked, turning around.

Zack was sitting in the beanbag chair. He looked shattered. He tried to speak, but choked on his words. Then, he cleared his throat and said, "I'm sorry, Sudi. I feel disgusted with myself." He rubbed his face with his hands.

Sudi ignored his apology. At the moment she didn't think she could ever stop feeling angry toward him. "You've got to get out of the cult, Zack."

He stood up, and when his hand reached out to touch her, she slapped it away.

"I don't have time to talk right now," she said hard-heartedly. She picked up her coat and grabbed her wand, determined to leave without saying another word; but then she caught the distress in his eyes, and her emotions softened. Part of her wished she could stay and talk to him, but she had something far more pressing to do. An atavistic instinct had awakened inside her and was urging her to hurry to another place.

She charged down the stairs without saying more.

"What now?" Meri asked, rushing beside her, her steps as loud as the thunder outside.

Dalila followed them. "Where are you going?"

"I'm not sure yet," Sudi replied as she jumped down the last three steps. Then another thought occurred to her, and she stopped abruptly, so that Meri tumbled into her. "I forgot to tell you thank you." She hugged Meri and Dalila fiercely. "How did you ever find me?"

"You called me and asked us to go over to your house," Meri said as they raced across the landing to the next flight of stairs. "Don't you remember?"

"I think your mother was surprised to see us on your porch with our wands," Dalila added.

"When she told us that you had gone over to Zack's to study," Meri continued, "we knew that you were in big trouble again."

"I was so stupid," Sudi said. "I realize that now. But at the time I thought I'd come over here and convince Zack to help me stop the ghost."

A few moments later, they stepped outside. Lightning bolts streaked through the clouds, making the night stutter between light and shadow. Thunder rattled the front windows of the house as the girls continued out to the street.

"So, where are we going?" Meri linked arms with Sudi.

"We're going to go fight the real danger." Sudi faced the wind-driven rain, feeling an odd urgency build inside her. "While the ghost possessed me, I was able to read her thoughts. The cult leader had convinced her that I was the one who wanted to destroy the cosmic harmony. That's why she turned against me."

"But if the ghost hasn't been stealing your

energy, then are you just . . ." Meri let her words trail off.

Laughing, Sudi finished the question for her: "Am I just incredibly incompetent and unable to train my wand?"

"I didn't want to say those words," Meri said. "But, yeah, is that the problem?"

"No, a ghost has definitely been stealing my power," Sudi answered. "But not the one we were blaming."

"Are you saying there are two ghosts?" Dalila asked.

"Yes." Sudi's answer echoed out into the storm. "When the cult leader discovered that I had brought a spirit back with me on the bracelet I stole from the tomb, he decided to use the ghost and Zack to distract me from the real danger. His plan almost succeeded."

"Two ghosts? Are you certain?" Dalila asked. Her tone implied that she didn't believe Sudi. "Because the ghost we just dealt with didn't want to leave your body."

"I know." Sudi sighed, remembering Zack's kiss. "She wanted to feel the pleasures of having a body again, and Zack is gorgeous."

"No doubt about that," Meri agreed.

"I can't believe it took me so long to figure out who the real threat is," Sudi said when they reached the corner. Headlights from an oncoming car shone upon them and reflected off the rain-slick street.

Meri and Dalila waited for her to continue.

"My sisters' Ouija board had said *a* bracelet, not *my* bracelet, had caused the manifestation of the ghost. I think the spirit of one of the dangerous dead came back with Carter's bracelet when Dalila's uncle brought it back from Egypt about two weeks ago, because that's about the time that Raul started going to my school."

"Raul?" Meri exclaimed. "He's as real as you or me. You said you kissed him, and you couldn't have done that with a ghost."

"He's the *mut*," Sudi said firmly.

"I think you're wrong," Dalila argued. "A ghost doesn't drive a Maserati."

"True," Sudi said. "Unless he conjured it."

"No way," Meri said.

"Yes, way," Sudi answered. "And Isis even told

me through Brian that night outside my house—"

"When Brian was helping you break into the basement?" Dalila asked.

"Exactly," Sudi answered. "Brian told me *matter is nothing more than a manifestation of energy*. At the time, I just thought he was being his annoying self, telling me something he'd learned in physics, but I'm sure it was a clue from Isis, and if I'd listened and thought about what happened that night, I would have been able to figure it out right then. Because when I ran my hand over the dashboard of Raul's car, this weird powder came off on my fingers—not dust exactly, more like grit."

"Or like magic residue," Dalila said authoritatively, doubt no longer lingering in her tone.

"You mean he drove a car that wasn't real?" Meri asked, awestruck.

"Yes, I'm sure now it wasn't real," Sudi said. "And that's what Isis was trying to tell me, but I was so focused on Zack, and so afraid of him, that I dismissed the clue."

"That's exactly what the cult wanted you to do," Dalila said. "Now I understand how they were using Zack to distract you."

"But even without that hint from Isis, I should have known," Sudi said, blaming herself. "Enough things had happened already to clue me in."

"Like what?" Meri asked.

"When my sisters accidentally threw salt on Raul, he freaked out," Sudi said. "At the time, I just assumed that he'd gotten salt in his eyes."

"The salt was most likely corroding his manifestation," Dalila explained. "Special salts will stop a ghost."

They walked in silence, past the next three houses, their wands tapping in harmony on the concrete.

Then, quietly, Sudi said, "Raul was always glancing at his watch like he needed to keep track of the time and that night at the club, right when we were having the best time ever, he glanced at his watch and said he had to leave."

"Because he has time limits on his magic," Dalila guessed.

"You mean like Cinderella at the ball?" Meri asked. "He had to take you home before the spell he'd used to conjure the Maserati wound down.

"Exactly," Sudi said.

"His car was going to change back into a pumpkin." Meri started laughing.

Dalila put an arm around Meri to quiet her before she spoke. "So what he conjures disintegrates, and apparently at a rapid pace. His magic is not long-lasting, and if that's true, if he does have a time limit on his magic, then that shows a weakness. He's not all-powerful."

"Not yet, anyway," Meri said unhappily, "because so far, he hasn't been able to steal all of Sudi's power."

Lightning lit the sky. The gentle rain became a sudden downpour that sent them racing to shelter under a nearby bus stop. Water pummeled the glass overhead.

"Every time I saw Raul his resemblance to Scott was stronger. I should have at least thought that was odd."

"You were falling in love," Meri said. "It could have happened to any one of us, but something else bothers me. Raul could have resembled anyone, but he chose Scott. How could he know you were attracted to Scott unless he had been following you for some time before he appeared?"

"That explains the shadow in the hallway that was chasing you," Dalila said. "You thought it was Zack and his friends, but I'm confident it was Raul."

"I'm sure it was," Sudi agreed as the rain eased enough for them to leave the shelter. "Do you remember my fantasy about wanting to be the bad one in a relationship?"

"Did he give you that, too?" Meri asked, splashing through a puddle.

"He made me believe that I was his first kiss," Sudi replied as an uneasy feeling came over her. "I don't understand why Isis doesn't just tell us straight out what we need to know."

"I agree," Meri said, disgruntled. "I mean, why all the mystery, like speaking through Brian? Just tell us!"

"I've been thinking about that," Dalila said, remaining serene. "If you consider the infinite size of the universe, then what has been happening to us is small compared to what could happen. I think Isis is preparing us so we'll be strong enough to face what is coming."

"That thought doesn't cheer me up," Meri said. "If this is the small stuff, then the coming battles must be humongous, like the last stand between good and evil."

"The ancients imagined an apocalyptic end, with the universe returning to the way it was before time began," Dalila explained. "Atum and Osiris would be the only survivors, and they would start the world again."

"Well, if it's supposed to end anyway, why do they need us?" Sudi asked petulantly.

"We're here to make sure that Seth isn't the last god standing," Dalila surmised.

Remembering something she had forgotten until that moment, Sudi groaned and gingerly touched her temple. She hated the way her fingers had already begun to tremble.

"What is it?" Dalila asked, her wand held out in a defensive pose.

"That night when I left Abdel's house feeling so down, I was wishing that I could go dancing in one of the outlaw clubs with my old dance crew, Emily and Nana. When I ran into Raul, he wanted to take me out and—"

"—That's where he took you," Meri finished for her.

"So he must be in my mind." Sudi felt dizzy with fear.

Dalila looked stricken. "At the very least, he's able to read your thoughts, even from far away."

Quickening her pace, Sudi said, "That means he already knows that we're on our way to him."

CHAPTER 24

Mud squished under Sudi's boots as she dashed forward. The rich smells of wet earth and grass rose into the rain.

"How do you know where to find Raul?" Meri asked as she raced along beside her.

Sudi stopped. "That's odd," she stammered, suddenly disoriented and adrift. "Before you asked, I thought I knew where I was going. Now I'm not sure."

"Maybe Raul entranced you," Meri suggested. "Do you think he's nearby?" Vigilant and alert, she looked left, then right, appearing to search for Raul in the shadows.

"I don't think that was it." Sudi shook her head. "Whatever it was, it didn't feel like it wanted to harm me or control me. It was trying to help me."

Dalila joined them. "Did you have confidence that someone was guiding you?"

"Yes, like guides were walking beside me, pulling me forward," Sudi said, wonder-struck. "I had a sense of knowing, but it's gone now."

"You were using the old way," Dalila explained. "We're descended from people who were forced to find their way in a like manner."

"What do you mean?" Sudi asked as Dalila gently turned her back in the direction she had been going.

"I'll explain, but first we need to press on." Dalila nudged Sudi forward. "You mustn't think, or you will become lost."

Squinting into the rain, Sudi gazed at the lights reflected off the wet pavement and tried to clear her mind. Gradually, magic took hold again and pulled her north across the street. As she increased her pace, Dalila fell into step beside her, and Meri joined them, her teeth chattering noisily.

"This is what my uncle told me," Dalila began. "Centuries ago, worshipping the old gods and practicing magic became illegal. Soon after that, people forgot that magic was real and benevolent. They learned to fear it and think of it as evil. Authorities called its practice heresy. They tortured and executed magicians and sorcerers."

"But we don't learn about that in history," Meri said skeptically.

"Of course not," Dalila said. "The crimes against those who kept the old ways were so horrific that what was done to them was never recorded. Besides, no one would believe the stories of their plight, because no one today believes that magic is real. But what happened to our ancestors is real."

"Our ancestors?" Sudi asked. "I thought we were descended from the pharaohs."

"We are, but after Cleopatra, the pharaohs no longer reigned. Her death marked the end of the pharaohs, and our way fell into disrepute. Our ancestors had to keep their identities hidden, for fear of persecution. They were forced into hiding, and when they needed to meet, they couldn't send out invitations or announce a gathering. That was far too dangerous. So the elders cast a spell that still encircles the world today. When a meeting of any kind is called, those who have a need to be there intuitively find their way to the right place."

"So you're saying that Sudi *knows* how to find Raul, because she is supposed to meet him," Meri said.

"Because she wants to confront him, she will find him," Dalila explained.

"Wow," Meri exclaimed. "It's like our own Global Positioning System."

"Yeah," Sudi muttered glumly. "One that leads us to demons and the very people who want to kill us."

At the crossroads, Sudi paused and stared out at the storm. Turbulent winds made sheets of rain turn into eddies that circled down the pavement.

Sudi pointed, astonished by her sense of knowing. "We need to go that way another block, across from the large apartment building, to the condemned row houses."

They set off again, wading through the water that had surged over the gutters and onto the sidewalk.

A sudden intense gust blew around the trees. The scraggy branches bent back and forth, making thin shadows that jumped and twitched around them. With her side vision, Sudi caught a glimpse within the movement of something dark and foreboding sliding sinuously after them. She froze, suddenly afraid. When she turned to face the shadow, it vanished, with a swiftness that seemed impossible.

"Where did it go?" Dalila stepped forward, her wand pointed at the ground where the shadow had been moments before.

Immediately, a slick swoosh came from behind them. The sound set Sudi on edge. She spun around in time to see the black form glide across the grass before disappearing again.

"What was it?" Meri whispered, pinching Sudi's arm.

"The dangerous dead," Sudi replied, unable to ignore the creeping feeling that the shadow was still nearby, watching them. She felt the same prickly feeling on her back and shoulders that she had felt in the hallways at school when the phantom shadow had been stalking her.

CHAPTER 25

Lightning lit the sky, and thunder followed immediately, the vibration rumbling through the ground. The storm slammed into Sudi with more force than before.

"Over there," Dalila said. Sparks sputtered from the end of her wand. The twinkling light silvered the raindrops and gave the night an eerie glow. The tiny stars spun over to the building and lit the darkness near the foundation.

Something dark and blurry clung to the brick

wall. It reared up, then flew at them, a spider-shape, shooting out spiraling threads.

Meri screamed and lifted her wand, muttering words that Sudi couldn't hear. Light shot out and enveloped the spidery silhouette. The form fell and hit the ground with a thud.

"Did we get him that easily?" Sudi stared down at the strange tentacles now thrashing in a puddle as they began to dissolve.

"No," Dalila said. "Raul got away before Meri's magic even touched the creature he conjured. He's only sparring with us to test our magic."

"If he's just going through the motions now, then I don't want to see what the real fight is like," Sudi said, feeling overwhelmed.

"Over there," Meri whispered sharply. "I keep seeing something near the porch."

Sudi glanced that way. A dark shape hunkered down in the corner. "Maybe it's just a pile of trash."

But as she spoke, it moved, skulking closer, a sinister black shadow.

"A ghost is supposed to be sheer and thin and see-through, not solid and black," Meri said in a hushed voice before taking a shuddering breath. "It looks like tar gliding over the water."

"This isn't an ordinary ghost. It's one of the dangerous dead," Dalila whispered. "After death he defied the gods and refused to pass on to the afterworld, where he would be judged."

"And we're supposed to fight him when he has that kind of power?" Meri asked. In the circle of amber light cast from the streetlamp, she looked ready to cry. Slowly, she removed her gloves, then took off her coat and let it fall onto the ground. She held her wand with both hands, battle ready.

Sudi could feel the trembling in her own wand, its apprehension matching her own. Her waterlogged coat had become a heavy weight on her shoulders. Following Meri's lead, she slipped it off.

"Do we know how to attack him?" Meri whispered.

"We have the curses from the Execration Texts." Dalila stripped off her coat and patted her jeans pocket. "So, on the count of three, we'll face him. Use your wands to block and contain him while I recite the words."

The shadow vanished.

"I think he overheard us," Sudi whispered. "I hope that means he's afraid of the curses."

"Maybe." Dalila looked around. "Or it could be that he's decided to attack us before we can use the curses."

A sudden chill raced up Sudi's back, and in the same moment, she sensed that something was terribly wrong. She looked behind her, not sure what she expected to see, but even though she saw nothing threatening, the feeling of danger did not go away.

In the distance, an engine revved up. Moments later, a car rounded the corner. Light from the front of the vehicle swept over them before shining back on the street.

Sudi blinked furiously, trying to readjust her vision to the darkness. Her fear had reached a new level. Suddenly, with a burst of adrenaline, she knew what was wrong.

"The car!" she gasped. "It's a Maserati!"

At once the car jounced over the curb and sped toward them, its rear tires spraying mud in high arcs up into the air.

Sudi sprinted away, trying to remember a

spell to cast with her wand, but her mind was blank.

Beside her, Dalila ran clumsily. Sparks sputtered from her wand but did nothing to slow the car down.

"I can't remember a thing that Abdel taught us!" Meri yelled in a panicked voice.

Ahead of them, the lights of the car bounced over the row houses. When the girls veered to the right, the mud caught them, sucking their feet down. Sudi staggered forward as Dalila stumbled and fell in front of her. She landed hard and slid across the rain-drenched soil.

"Go on without me," Dalila ordered.

"No way," Meri said, grabbing her arm.

The headlights blinded Sudi as she helped Dalila to her feet.

"Hold out your wands," Dalila said shakily as she wiped the mud off her own.

Meri pointed her wand and asked, "If the car's made of magic, can it kill us?"

"It felt real riding in it!" Sudi yelled back, trying to aim the tip of her wand at the car bearing down on them.

Dalila spoke the words of the spell. *"Se-hetem-na mut."*

"Destroy the dangerous dead!" Sudi shouted, repeating the words in English.

White sparks burst from all three wands and shot at the car, but when the sparks hit the hood, Raul's magic snuffed them out.

"Who's going to save the world now?" Sudi groaned.

"Get behind the wall!" Meri shouted, already running. Dalila limped after her.

Sudi threw herself over the crumbling bricks, the jagged edges scraping her hands. She landed with a dull thump between Meri and Dalila.

When the Maserati turned toward them, the fender swiped a tree. The blow was enough to send the wheels zigzagging off course. The car skidded sideways through the mud until the front end crashed into a fire hydrant, which exploded, sending a geyser of water into the air.

A lone hubcap flew off the smashed vehicle and bounced toward the girls. It hit the walkway behind them, then spun with an oddly hollow metallic sound before landing. Rain pinged on the chrome. The metal dissolved rapidly, the magic dregs washing down the sidewalk.

When Sudi glanced up, the car had already liquefied.

In the apartment building across the street, lights came on through the windows. Despite the rain, some residents ventured out onto their balconies in their pajamas, phones held at their ears, to see what had caused the noise.

Sirens filled the night.

"Let's get out of here before the police show up," Sudi said, her heart still racing. "We'll go through the alley to the back entrance of the house."

The girls started walking again, staying close to the buildings. When they reached the corner, a Metropolitan squad car pulled up to the curb alongside them.

"How am I ever going to explain this to my

mother?" Meri said, licking her swelling lip. "I'll be her biggest political liability."

"How can you worry about your mom's career right now?" Sudi scolded, but when she saw Meri's distressed expression, she quickly added, "Blame me. Say it's my fault you're here. Getting in trouble has become my way of life. I think my parents expect it."

Dalila linked arms with her friends. "Right now our problem is more immediate. We can't let anything delay us from what we need to do."

The policeman got out of the car, hitched up his utility belt, and sauntered to the back of the car. He flicked on a flashlight. The beam of light bobbed over the girls. After staring at each girl in turn, he slapped his hand on the trunk. "I want you young ladies to come over here and show me some ID."

Meri groaned.

"I'll figure out something," Dalila whispered. With a regal smile, she started toward the officer, pulling herself up to her full height. In spite of the mud covering her face and clothes, she had the bearing of a queen.

Sudi pinched her arm and yanked her back. "Wait. He's not a real cop," she warned.

Dalila whipped around. "You mean he's another conjuring?" she asked, clearly impressed. Then, studying the policeman, she said, "He looks real, but a good magician could do that."

Sudi and Dalila started to back away, pulling Meri with them, but she wouldn't move.

"It's bad enough for my mom if I get arrested," Meri said. "But it's twice as bad if I run from the cops. Are you positive?"

"For one thing, he should have stopped to put out road flares around the broken hydrant," Sudi whispered. "And even if he forgot to do that, everyone in D.C. knows who you are because of your mom. The cop should have called his captain as soon as he saw your face."

"Young ladies." The officer scowled at them. "I'm waiting."

Meri looked torn between running and following the officer's order.

"I was at a party that got busted," Sudi explained in a low voice. "A senator's daughter was with me. When we got caught, the first thing the cop did was call his captain. Dozens of officials came out to handle the arrest."

Meri still didn't budge.

"I know how we can find out," Dalila whispered. She aimed the tip of her wand at the officer.

A spray of stars burst into the rain, spiraling toward the policeman. He ducked, but not fast enough. Twinkling pinpricks of light embedded themselves in his forehead. Immediately, his skin began to melt into his eyes.

The officer raised his hand. Brightness flashed from his palm and grew, shimmering and expanding, casting the rain aside.

"He's going to throw a counterspell!" Dalila screamed.

"Run!" Meri yelled, already heading into the alley.

The air split above Sudi as she took off. The sound of the shock wave echoed into the storm louder than the peals of thunder. Her ears ached from the noise. She ducked behind a dilapidated garage and stood there shivering with her friends, her head pounding.

Suddenly, Raul materialized beside them.

Startled by his sudden appearance, Sudi gasped. Raul looked like Scott with a dangerous edge, his handsome features sharp, his smile cruel.

"The three of you are pathetic Descendants," Raul sneered. "You won't even stand and face me in battle, but, like whimpering cowards, you run. Why were you chosen?"

"You were the one following me in the hallway at school, weren't you?" Sudi countered with a question of her own.

"Are you only realizing that now?" he asked. "I can't believe how staggeringly dim-witted you are. You should have immediately known what I was, but instead you pined for me and yearned for my kisses." He leaned toward her now as if he were going to embrace her. She recoiled, feeling nauseated and dizzy from the evil that flowed from him.

"Are my kisses no longer desired by you?" he laughed. "You're a fool. Your head is filled with romance and silly thoughts."

"Don't listen to him," Meri said, her wand glowing and burbling with energy. "He's only angry with himself because he wasn't skillful enough to deceive you."

Raul eyed Meri with contempt and held up his palm. Power emanated from him, and even though Meri held her wand in a defensive pose, his magic forced her back. She stumbled against Dalila. The light from her wand grew dull and went out.

Immediately, Raul faced Sudi again and seized her wand. Sparks arced off the bronze. He dropped his hold and cried out. Acrid-smelling smoke rose from between his fingers. Stunned, he looked down at his hand and examined the blisters and burns covering his skin.

"Your magic is inept," he said scornfully. "But, as worthless as you are, you've been given a wand with terrible force. Why is that?"

"If she's so worthless, then why are you trying to steal her power?" Dalila countered.

"You're only trying to make her feel bad about herself to weaken her," Meri added. "That must mean you fear her."

Raul regarded the three girls with hatred. "Better to kill you now," he whispered coldly, "than to listen to your drivel."

Energy whirred about him. The air trembled,

and in response the raindrops swarmed chaotically, creating a maelstrom around him.

"Run!" Sudi screamed and started forward, her legs weak and wobbling.

Clumsily, Meri and Dalila raced down the alley after her.

Ducking low, they scrambled for shelter in an entranceway. The magic screamed over their heads. Sudi's wand clattered on the concrete as she crawled closer to Dalila and Meri.

"Get out the curses," Sudi said jaggedly.

Dalila dug into her jeans pocket and pulled out the paper. "The rain soaked through my jeans," she whispered, distraught, her eyes widening. She tried to unfold the drenched paper, but water had turned it to mush. "What are we going to do now?"

CHAPTER 27

"Give me Sudi's wand," Raul said in response to Dalila's question.

Warily, the girls got up and stepped out from their hiding place. Then, standing shoulder to shoulder, they drew courage from one another and lifted their wands in challenge. Silvery light burst from the end of Meri's wand and formed a cocoon, a magic shell around all three girls.

Undaunted, Raul walked toward them, his feet sloshing through the water. This time, when he reached for Sudi's wand, pulsing light formed a shield over his skin.

Meri and Dalila crossed their wands in front of him, blocking his outstretched hand. The clang of metal rang out and resounded around them.

Raul stepped back. Anger flashed across his face before he melted into a thick, black pool that slithered past them, up the back stairs, and into the abandoned row house. A curious scent of tombs and death wafted after him.

"Are we supposed to follow him?" Sudi asked. "Is that what he expects us to do?"

"You were guided to him tonight, so I assume that means he must be stopped now." Dalila gazed up at the clouds. "We can't see the stars, but terrible things could be happening in the heavens."

Meri chewed on her lip as she studied the rickety stairs leading up to the back entrance. "He's probably got the building fortified with magic that will weaken us as soon as we enter. Or maybe another conjuring is waiting to attack us at the threshold. He might have—"

"Stop." Sudi put her arm around Meri. "I'm

already scared. You don't need to give me more reasons to be afraid."

"I'll make us fearless," Dalila said and then spoke a spell for protection: *"Aha-a sexem a xesef-a madret-d."*

In the downpour, light shimmered and colored the raindrops orange. The protective glow ballooned out and surrounded all three girls.

A feeling of serenity came over Sudi, but when the light faded, fear broke through her tranquility, stronger than Dalila's magic.

"At least we'll be inside, out of the rain," Meri said glumly as they trudged up the stairs and entered the house.

Dim light from the street filtered through the cracks in the boarded-up windows. Cautiously, the girls traipsed through crumbled plaster and broken whiskey bottles. Rain had leaked through the roof. Water dripped noisily from the broken light fixtures and streamed in tiny rivulets down the walls. The moisture heightened the stench of rodents' nests, mildew, and decay.

When the girls stepped into the hallway, they stopped.

"It's too dark to go on," Sudi whispered.

Dalila pushed in front of her and spoke a singsong incantation. Immediately, blue flames licked the end of her wand and cast an eerie glow about the room.

"Even an apprentice magician knows how to make such pitiable light." Raul's disembodied voice came from above them. A sudden puff of air blew out the flames.

Meri moved closer to Sudi and pulled Dalila toward them. "How are we supposed to stop him without the curses from the Execration Texts?"

"Since our last encounter with a demon," Dalila whispered, "I've been studying incantations for sending evil creatures back to Duat. Maybe that will be enough."

"If he was strong enough to resist the gods and not go there after his death, then I don't think our magic will be strong enough," Sudi said. "Besides, I don't feel right about it."

"Do you care what happens to him?" Meri asked in a low voice. "I mean, he obviously wants to destroy you so he can use your wand."

"It's too late for discussion," Dalila said

impatiently. "I'm going to transform into Wadjet. As a cobra, I'll be able to sense Raul's location. Then maybe we can surprise him."

Sudi felt doubtful, but she didn't have a better plan.

Moments later, a spray of fire lit the room. Flames spat from the cobra's mouth. The snake's hood was spread in a defensive display.

"What's wrong?" Sudi asked, starting toward the reptile.

The cobra vanished before she reached it. In its place, small fires burned fitfully, sending acrid smoke into the moist air.

"What did he do to Dalila?" Meri clutched Sudi's arm, her wand spattering bits of light about the room. Purple embers stuck to the dilapidated walls and quickly went out.

"I don't know." Sudi's mouth felt dry, and when she spoke, her voice sounded hoarse. "Dalila!" she called out.

The scuffling sound of someone struggling came from the basement.

"Run!" Dalila cried, but her scream was cut off. A sigh followed, and then a soft thump.

"Come rescue your friend," Raul called out. "I thought I was killing a snake, but it turns out that the viper was Dalila."

"He knew," Meri said angrily.

"Of course he did," Sudi said, edging forward. Her fingers brushed over the exposed laths.

When she found the stairway to the basement, Meri grabbed her shoulders and stopped her from starting down the stairs.

"Only the top steps are there," Meri warned. "The rest have fallen away." Her eyes glowed yellow, like a cat's. "I didn't transform completely," she explained. "Only enough that I'd have feline vision." Unexpectedly, her hands slipped away from Sudi's shoulders. She screamed as an unseen force pulled her into the darkness, away from Sudi.

"Meri?" Sudi cried.

A moment later, Raul's voice came from the bottom of the stairwell. "Meri's with me, too. The only way you have to save your friends is to come down here and face me."

Clutching her wand against her chest, Sudi took a deep breath. Before she had even finished the incantation to transform, her wings unfurled.

Flapping them gently, she lifted her body, then alighted on the basement floor.

Something cold and tingly crawled over her skin. At first she thought cobwebs had caused the feeling, but then she realized Raul was standing next to her, his breath gently caressing her face.

"Lay down your wand," he said against her ear. "It's the only way to save your friends."

Defeated, Sudi started to put her wand down, then stopped. "I can't," she whimpered. "You'll use my wand to destroy the universe."

"I've read your thoughts," he said in a hushed, soothing tone. "I know that all you've ever wanted was to be an ordinary mortal, a party girl. Give me the wand, and you'll have your wish."

She shook her head fiercely. "Descendants who fail are sent to live with the demons in chaos," she said, tightening her grip on the wand.

His hand stroked her back, and she shivered in response, too terrified and weak to pull away from him. He chuckled, seeming to enjoy her distress. "Chaos isn't what you imagine it to be," he said. "The creatures there are pure evil, but, then, so am I, and you were able to love me."

"I loved a lie," she whispered back.

He pressed his fingers against her forehead. His raw power seeped into her, leaching what little energy she had left. When at last he drew his hand back, she could no longer hold herself up. She collapsed to her knees, grasping her wand with both hands.

Then, closing her eyes, she fell forward, vaguely aware that her wand was rolling away from her. Cold settled deep inside her, and with it came the strangest feeling that she was falling into herself, retracting, and becoming very small. Her heart slowed, the beats growing fainter in her ears.

The clanking of metal against concrete roused her. Groggily, she opened her eyes. Her wand, now in Raul's hands, glowed with power, its tip pointed at her face.

"I believe that you will be the first Descendant defeated by her own wand," Raul said victoriously.

Magic shot out from the wand. A brilliant light looped around her. Every time she exhaled, the coils tightened, preventing her from taking in air until finally she surrendered, and blackness swept her away.

CHAPTER 28

Intense pain was still raging inside Sudi when she opened her eyes to a dream world. She was no longer in the basement of the abandoned house, but somewhere deep inside herself. A bewildering array of images rushed around her, nightmare pictures of a storm.

She tried to sit up to see better, but dizziness pushed her back against someone. Gentle hands were holding her. She turned her head and breathed in the scent of a sweet perfume. Isis was sitting beside her, cradling her. The nimbus that encircled the goddess lit the space surrounding them.

"It's time to arise, Sudi," Isis whispered. "You are the only one who can stop Raul now."

"But how?" Sudi asked. "Tell me what to do."

"Why should I tell you when he already has?" Isis asked.

"He couldn't have told me," Sudi insisted. "I'd remember something that important. And even if I knew, I don't have enough strength left to fight him."

"Of course, you do," Isis whispered. "*Senf en Auset.* The blood of Isis flows through your veins."

The goddess kissed Sudi's forehead in the exact spot where Raul had touched her moments before to drain her power.

"Try to remember." Isis disappeared, leaving Sudi alone in the surreal world.

Surrendering to the pain again, Sudi lay motionless. She dismissed the conversation as delirium, nothing more than a hallucination brought about by the death jolt of her own wand. But within her sleep, she remembered that Abdel had once told her that the ancient Egyptians believed that the gods spoke to the pharaoh through dreams. She tried to rouse herself and think. What had Raul told her that might give her the key to stopping him?

When the answer came to her, she forced herself back into consciousness. Her awakening breath came with an explosion of pain. She was surprised to find herself standing outside in the storm, near the toppled fire hydrant. Apparently, the emergency vehicles had come and stopped the surging water.

She glanced up. The clouds had taken on a strange green cast. Large hail began to fall, pelting her at the same time that rain poured down on her, but she didn't run for shelter. She was too spellbound by the nearly continuous display of lightning. She heard Raul and turned sharply.

"*Maaxera!*" He shouted his triumph. A fiery light burned in her wand as he held it high above his head. From the tip of her wand, spidery electrical veins flashed in the sky.

She knew he was casting the spells that would allow him to return to the past and, from that vantage point in time, destroy the world.

"I've come to take my wand back," Sudi said, her voice small, filled with terror.

He looked down at her, obviously surprised to see her standing before him.

"You have nothing, not even your shadow." He laughed derisively. "And you expect me to surrender such power to you?" He aimed the wand at her and sent out an invisible burst of power that pushed her back.

Even though her body was racked with new pain, she walked toward him again. "I know how to defeat you, because you told me what to do."

He started to laugh again, then stopped, appearing uncertain, before his confidence returned. "I have your power. You can't defeat me."

When he aimed her wand at her again, she was determined not to give him the pleasure of her fear. She didn't cower but eased closer to him, even though her knees were wobbling.

"You didn't take my power," she said. "You can't take something that doesn't belong to me. My true power comes through me, but it belongs to the stars."

Crazed with anger, he pointed the wand at her

again. When the energy shot out at her, she was ready. She stepped aside and dodged the attack.

"That first night when you came over to my house," she said, "you told my sisters that they should be concerned about the ghost because maybe it wanted them to help it pass on. I think you were projecting your own desire onto the ghost."

"Nonsense," he answered. "It was only something I said to entertain your silly sisters."

Ignoring his comment, Sudi defiantly stepped closer to him. "I'll help you pass on to the other side."

Before he could answer, she raised her hands to the sky. Wind whipped violently around her.

"Force of the stars, I offer these words," Sudi said. "*Sexem-a.* Let me have power. *Xut en Auset.* The power of Isis."

At first she thought the trembling of the earth beneath her feet was only the reverberation of thunder, but she soon realized that the power coming into her was what was making the ground quake.

Sudi stretched out her arm, her two fingers

pointed at the wand, in the way Abdel had taught her. With a speed that seemed impossible, her wand flew back to her. She caught it and raised it in tribute to the stars.

Raul watched her, his handsome face appealing and seductive. Even though she knew what he was, she held his gaze, captivated. It had been easy to love him, so there must have been something good inside him. Staring at him now, she also sensed his terrible sorrow and his regret for what he had done in life.

Unexpectedly, Meri and Dalila ran from the house, racing toward her through the wind-driven rain and hail.

"What did you do to make his magic release us?" Meri said. Then she saw Raul and added, "Why are you stopping? He'll regain his power."

"Speak the words," Dalila urged. "Quickly, before he does something."

Sudi recalled another demon that she had sent back to live in the primeval darkness of the world before creation. She had pitied the demon for what she had done to it, and she had wished that she had spoken other words to save its soul. This was what she intended to do now, for Raul.

"I'm going to try another way," Sudi said.

"Someone as evil as he is can only be destroyed," Dalila cautioned. "You can't save him."

But Sudi followed her heart. Lifting her wand above her head, she prayed to the universe to guide her. "I speak these terrible words of power," she said at last. "Pierce the heart of this one here and dispel the darkness. Free his spirit from the evil that holds him. Let him pass on to live in the kingdom of Duat, the dwelling place of the gods."

Spears of lightning shot across the night sky and entwined themselves in one massive bolt that struck the end of Sudi's wand. The force shivered through her; not the heat, but the unstoppable power of the universe. A concussion boomed through the earth as she pointed the wand at Raul. Light raced from the end and struck him. He staggered back, his face a rictus of fear. As white fire consumed him, his eyes filled with gratitude, the fear gone. He disappeared, and only the unearthly blaze remained.

Sudi stared at her friends, exhausted. They grabbed her arms as she started to fall.

Tattered and bruised, Meri embraced her. "You did it."

"No, not me," Sudi said, gazing up at the clearing sky. "It was his spirit's longing for the light. Remember when we went down to Apep's lair, that feeling of utter hopelessness without God?"

"The condemned are denied the presence of God," Dalila said.

"I think he regretted what he had done in life and that was his real reason for not going to Duat after his death. He didn't want to create havoc in this world. He wanted to find forgiveness, so he could return home to eternity."

"But then the cult caught him," Meri said.

They started walking home, crunching over the hail and slogging through the puddles.

"But how did you figure out that he wanted your help?" Dalila asked.

"When he found out that my sisters were exorcising a ghost," Sudi said, "he told them that maybe the ghost was trying to get their attention, because it wanted their help."

"Do you think that's true for the other ghost?" Meri asked. "The one trying to possess your body?"

Sudi nodded. "That ghost is a good spirit. I can take care of her alone."

Later that night, Sudi awakened with a start. The ghost hovered above her.

"Mistress, I've come to apologize," the ghost whispered. "While I was inside your body, I realized that the cult leader had lied to me. You are pure good. It was never my intention to harm you."

"I know," Sudi answered. "I could read your thoughts, also, while you were inside me."

The ghost giggled and cuddled against Sudi. Her touch felt like a gentle breeze swaying back and forth. "I didn't want to leave your body, mistress. Please forgive me. But it was such joy to feel so many sensations again."

"I understand," Sudi whispered.

Then the ghost pulled back and uncurled her fist, revealing a dark ball. "I've brought your shadow back to you."

A silhouette—Sudi's own—grew from the ball and sprang about the room before attaching itself to Sudi.

"I'm weary, mistress," the ghost said. "How am I to go home?"

"Isis will help you," Sudi replied.

A light spiraled down in front of them. Within it, golden wings materialized and unfolded, revealing the goddess Isis in her avian form.

"I am Isis. She of many names. I have come to take you home." Isis gently took the bracelet from Sudi's arm. She cradled the ghost against her. "My husband, Osiris, who is king of the dead, awaits you."

Sudi opened her bedroom window.

Isis drifted out, holding the ghost tightly. Then her wings caught the air and lifted her above the treetops. Sudi sat on the windowsill, watching them. On impulse, she snapped out her wings and flew after Isis.

The rain had stopped. Moonlight silvered the scudding clouds and cast a milky light across the houses below. The stars were no longer clustered oddly but once again twinkled in their familiar places in the night sky.

When Isis released the ghost, she soared up, a stream of light, until she became a star, one of the blessed dead, shining down brightly on Sudi.

Her confidence restored, Sudi flew out across the city. She no longer had to fear what her life had become.